Christmas
at
Mountain View
Lodge

Deanna Lynn Sletten

Christmas at Mountain View Lodge

Copyright 2023 © Deanna Lynn Sletten

ISBN-13: 978-1-941212-76-9

Cover Designer: Deborah Bradseth

Novels by

Deanna Lynn Sletten

WOMEN'S FICTION

Night Music

One Wrong Turn

Finding Libbie

Maggie's Turn

Summer of the Loon

Memories

Widow, Virgin, Whore

HISTORICAL FICTION

Mrs. Winchester's Biographer

The Secrets We Carry

The Ones We Leave Behind

The Women of Great Heron Lake

Miss Etta

MURDER/MYSTERY

Rachel Emery Series

The Truth About Rachel

Death Becomes You

ROMANCE

Destination Wedding

Sara's Promise

Lake Harriet Series

Under the Apple Blossoms

Chasing Bailey

As the Snow Fell

Walking Sam

Kiss a Cowboy Series

Kiss a Cowboy

A Kiss for Colt

Kissing Carly

HOLIDAY FICTION

The Christmas Charm

Christmas at Mountain View Lodge

YOUNG ADULT

Outlaw Heroes

Christmas

at
Mountain View
Lodge

Chapter One

Summer - 1965

Edna Burke and her husband Arnie were having a wonderful time vacationing at Big Bear Lake, California. The children enjoyed playing in the bright blue water, and they had also hiked one of the many trails in the forest. It was so peaceful compared to the coastal town they lived in just outside of Los Angeles. When Arnie first mentioned taking a trip to the mountains, Edna wasn't too excited. But now, she was glad they had.

She and the children, Amanda, age three, and Craig, age five, had spent the morning on the beach at the lake and had just returned to the small hotel room they'd rented nearby. Arnie had wanted to explore the town, and she'd been happy to let him. Edna knew that Arnie missed small-town living. He'd grown up in rural Michigan and had moved to California when he'd joined the military. But after a decade of living in the city, he was getting restless. Edna figured if she let him enjoy his vacation here, he might go home feeling more content.

Edna and the children had just reached the hotel when Arnie drove up in his 1957 Ford Custom sedan. He had a smile on his face as he stepped out of the car.

"You look happy," Edna said, fumbling with the key to open the hotel room door.

"Here, let me," Arnie said, taking the key. He unlocked the door, and the kids rushed inside. "I have something I want to show you," he told Edna.

"Right now?" she asked. "I need to change out of my swim-suit first and fix my hair."

"You look adorable just the way you are," Arnie said, steal-ing a kiss from her.

"My, my. You're in a good mood," Edna said, smiling. "But I do need to change before we go anywhere. And I have to get the kids dressed, too."

"Okay. But let's hurry. I can't wait to show you," Arnie said.

They walked into the small hotel room where they'd spent the last five days. There were two full-sized beds and a tiny bathroom. Arnie helped Craig dress while Edna corralled little Amanda and changed her clothes. Then Edna went into the bathroom to change. A few minutes later, she came out in a soft yellow cotton dress and flats.

"My hair is a mess," she said. Typically, she curled the ends of her straight blond hair, but the lake, wind, and sun had taken all the curl out of it.

"You look fine," Arnie said, looking anxious to get going.

"You're just saying that so we can leave," she told him. Quickly, she pulled her hair up into a ponytail. "This will have to do," she said, sighing.

They all piled into the car. Edna glanced over at Arnie. He looked so handsome with his dark, wavy hair a bit longer than usual and the golden tan he'd acquired this week at the lake. They'd been married for seven years, but he still looked like the young, gregarious man she'd met in 1957.

"Are we going for ice cream?" Craig asked from the back seat.

Arnie chuckled. "Maybe after dinner, son. But first, I want to show your mother something."

They drove east, away from the lake, and were soon out of town. There were pine trees everywhere, and Edna saw the cleared trails up the mountain where the ski resort was. Arnie turned left into a dirt parking lot and stopped in front of a large log building that looked deserted.

"Where are we?" Edna asked, gazing at the old building.

"This used to be an old saloon with rooms upstairs," Arnie said. "Come on. I want to show you how it looks inside."

Tentatively, Edna stepped out of the car as Arnie opened the back door so Craig and Amanda could crawl out. She turned to Arnie. "Why are we looking at this?"

Arnie's eyes flashed with excitement. "Because I think it would be the perfect building to turn into a resort."

"What?" Edna stared at him in disbelief. Had she heard wrong? "Why would we want to turn it into a resort?"

Arnie stepped up in front of Edna and gently placed his hands on her arms. "Please, just hear me out. I saw this place for sale today, and I had to see it. The real estate agent showed it to me while you and the kids were at the lake. It's rough, but it has so much potential. We could build up a business here, something we'd never be able to do in Los Angeles."

Edna felt like she'd been sideswiped. "But we don't live here, Arnie. We live in Los Angeles."

"I know. But we could live here. Don't you just love this town? It's beautiful here, and the people are so friendly. It would be the perfect place to raise children and grow our life."

"I'm confused," Edna said, frowning. "When did we decide we wanted to move here?"

"I know this is a lot to take in," Arnie said. "But please, come look at the building with me, and then we can talk. Please?"

"Do I have a choice?" Edna asked. But when she looked into Arnie's pleading eyes, she gave in with a sigh. "Okay. I'll look."

His face broke out into a boyish grin. "Great! The real estate agent gave me a key so I could show you. Come on."

The kids were already on the front porch, peering through one of the large, dirty windows on each side of the door. Arnie unlocked the rustic old lock and opened the door. Inside, it was dark, and a moldy smell rushed out at Edna before she even walked in.

"It's just been closed up for a long time," Arnie said. "Once it's aired out, the smell will go away."

Edna wasn't as sure but kept quiet. The kids rushed inside the large open room, and Edna slowly followed. It took a moment for her eyes to adjust to the dimness.

"The electricity isn't on, but it is hooked up. There haven't been any owners for a few years, so they shut it off," Arnie said. He pulled something out of his chino's pocket. "Lucky for you, I have a flashlight."

Edna glanced around the wide-open space as Arnie flashed the light. The ceiling was high with exposed log beams. There was a long bar across from the entrance with mirrors and shelves behind it. Wooden tables and chairs were stacked on the right side of the room. On the far left side of the room was a wooden staircase, and when she glanced up, Edna saw a balcony the entire length of the building.

"See up there?" Arnie said excitedly. "There are six bedrooms and two washrooms with running water. They'd be perfect for renting to guests. We could use a portion of the old bar as the front desk, and this room could be used as a combination dining room and living room." He flashed the light to the far right of the room. "There's a beautiful stone fireplace over there. Do you see it?"

Edna did see it. The fireplace was impressive, but the bear's head mounted above it gave her the willies. She turned to Arnie. "Why would we need a dining room?"

"For the guests," he said.

"You expect me to cook for everyone, too?"

"Well, maybe at first," Arnie said, wavering. "I mean, if we bought this place right now, we could have it ready for hunters by winter, and you'd probably have to cook them breakfast and supper. But as we fix the place up, we could eventually have families as guests, and then we could just serve a small breakfast each day."

Edna stared at him in disbelief. "Hunters?"

He grinned. "Only until we get started. Just think, though. As we fix the place up, it will be fancier and have better accommodations. Then we'll attract families all year round as well as skiers. And maybe hunters, too. But at first, only men hunting would probably want to stay here."

Edna continued staring at her husband, trying to grasp what he was saying. The kids were running around the large empty room, their footsteps echoing on the wood plank floor. Did he really expect them to pull up roots and move here?

"Come on, sweetheart. Let me show you the kitchen," Arnie said, taking her hand and pulling her toward a swinging door on the left side of the bar. "Come with us, kids," he called.

They all went into the large kitchen. There was a big gas stove and griddle, plus a walk-in freezer and refrigerator. In the middle of the room was a long butcherblock island that could be used for prep work.

"The real estate agent told me the last owners remodeled the kitchen. Isn't it nice?" Arnie asked.

Edna agreed it was nice for a commercial kitchen. But did she want to spend all her days in here cooking for strangers?

Arnie watched her eagerly, waiting for her reply. But Edna kept quiet. This was too much to absorb at once.

"I'll show you the upstairs," he said, leading the way with his flashlight.

Edna and the kids followed behind. The stairs were made of logs cut in half, and the railing was a long, thick log also. They went to the top, where there was a narrow hallway and several doors leading to rooms. From up here, you could see down into the open room below.

Arnie opened the door of one of the rooms. "They aren't too bad," he said, letting Edna walk past him into the room.

The room smelled musty, too. Two full-sized beds sat in the room with an end table between them. There was a dresser and a desk on the opposite wall. The room looked like the hotel room they were renting now, except there was no private bathroom.

"Are they all this size?" Edna asked, trying hard to show interest.

Arnie nodded his head. "Yes. I'll show you the bathrooms, too." He led her and the children to the next door and opened it. The bathroom was small but had a sink, toilet, and bathtub with a shower. The tile and tub needed a good scrubbing. "There are two of these up here," Arnie said. "It's perfect for hunters because they don't mind sharing a bathroom."

Edna cringed inside but kept quiet. She knew she'd be the one who'd have to clean up after the hunters.

They walked back downstairs, the kids running ahead of the adults.

"Kids! Be careful! Edna called after them. She didn't like how open the stairs were. The kids could fall and slide right through them.

They stepped outside onto the covered plank porch. Edna turned to Arnie. "Are we supposed to live in those rooms upstairs too?"

Arnie grinned. "Nope. I'll show you." He called to the kids. "Come with us, kids!" Arnie led them around to the back of the building, and out in the distance stood a cute cottage. "This place sits on ten acres. That cottage back here would be perfect for us until we build our own house on the property."

Edna sighed as they neared the cottage. It was cute, like something out of a fairy tale. But it was rustic, like the old bar. It was a log building with a dark green shingled roof and a wooden dark green door. She watched Arnie unlock the front door and followed him and the children inside. They walked directly into a small living room where a bay window faced the saloon, and a stone fireplace sat on the adjacent wall. An open doorway led to a kitchen that at least looked clean and had newer appliances. There was also a space for a washer and dryer in the back corner. Another doorway led out of the kitchen into a hallway. There were three small bedrooms and a bathroom down the hallway.

"It's cute, right?" Arnie asked Edna. "We've been saving for a house to get out of that apartment. We'd never get a house as big as this in Los Angeles."

"It is cute," Edna agreed grudgingly. "But I hadn't planned on buying a house and a lodge at the same time."

Arnie came up beside her and placed his arm around her small waist. "I know this isn't what we planned," he said. "But the moment I saw this place, I knew it was right. We can run our own business, and I won't have to work for someone else anymore."

She turned to face him. "I know it sounds good, but running your own business means working twenty-four hours a day. It'll be harder than having a job. And we both will have to work at it."

"But we can build something for ourselves," Arnie said. "Eventually, we'll have employees and won't have to work so hard."

Edna sighed. This was too much to think about all at once. "The kids are probably hungry after playing in the water all day. Let's eat dinner, and we can talk about it some more."

This made Arnie smile. "Okay."

They locked up the place and piled the kids in the backseat of the car. Arnie drove downtown to a local café that served homestyle meals. They'd eaten dinner there most of the nights they'd been in town because the food was so good.

Once they were seated and ordered, Arnie looked expectantly at Edna across the table. Craig sat beside him in the booth, and Amanda sat beside Edna. Both kids were drawing on their placemats with crayons the waitress had given them.

"So, what do you think?" Arnie asked eagerly. "Can you imagine us living here and having our own business?"

"I still don't know, honey," Edna said. "I always assumed we'd live in southern California near the beach and someday own a house there. That's what we were planning when we married and started saving for a house. Moving here was never something we even thought about."

Arnie reached across the table and held Edna's hands. "I know, baby. And I never thought of anything like this before, either, but this place just feels right. I miss living in the country. And I want our kids to have a small-town upbringing. This could be good for all of us."

"Can I at least have some time to think about it?" Edna asked.

Arnie opened his mouth to say something, then stopped. Finally, he nodded. "Sure, honey. We can wait a little while."

She smiled at him, relieved he didn't expect her to make a life-altering decision tonight.

The family ate, and afterward, they picked up ice cream at the Frosty Freeze down the road before returning to the hotel. By the time the kids had their baths and crawled into bed, they were so exhausted they fell asleep immediately.

After showering, Edna slid into bed with Arnie. His breathing was steady, so she assumed he was asleep. As she lay there, all she could think about was the lodge and how much Arnie wanted to buy it. She didn't believe he understood how much work it would be to own a business like that. And how much work it would be for her. She'd have to cook for everyone, clean the rooms daily, and do loads of laundry. On top of that, she would have to watch the children, too. Edna wasn't sure she wanted to commit to all that.

"Are you awake?" Arnie whispered.

"Yes," Edna answered. Not only was she thinking about how much work the lodge would be, but also about leaving her family and friends behind if they left Los Angeles. Her aging parents probably wouldn't make the trip to Big Bear to see

them and the children. And her friends, women she'd known
since grade school, probably wouldn't either. Like her, they
were at the beginning of growing their families and were busy.

"What are you thinking?" Arnie asked.

Edna sighed. "About everything I'd have to give up if we
moved here."

"I've thought of that, too," Arnie said. "I know you'd miss
your parents and your siblings. And your friends, too. It would
be a big adjustment for you."

Edna thought about how Arnie hadn't seen his parents
since joining the service. His parents couldn't afford to come
to California from Michigan, and neither could his siblings.
And they'd never been able to afford to go there, either. He'd
given up a lot when he'd married her and stayed in California.
But he'd never complained.

"It would be a big change," Edna said. "But you never see
your family, either. That must be hard."

Arnie rolled onto his side and looked at her. "I don't mind
as long as I'm with you."

Edna turned toward him. "Is this really something you
want?"

He nodded. "I've been thinking about opening my own
carpentry business for a long time, but we just don't have the
money. And we'd never be able to open any other business in
Los Angeles because there's too much competition. Here, we
could do well, I'm sure of it."

"You never said anything to me before about wanting your
own business," Edna said.

"That's because I didn't want you to feel bad that I wasn't
happy where I was working. I have to support you and the
kids—I want to support you. But I'm not happy in the city, and

having a boss stinks. But I'll continue to work and live there if that's what you want." Arnie reached his hand over and cupped her face. "I only want to make you happy."

Edna felt bad. She hadn't known Arnie was unhappy with his job. She knew he didn't like the city, but he'd never actually told her that. He'd worked so hard over the past few years supporting them. He was a good husband and father. She didn't want him to be unhappy just so she'd have what she wanted.

"If moving here and buying the lodge is really what you want, then I'm okay with it," Edna said. "It'll be a lot of work, but with your carpentry skills, I'm sure you can make it a really nice place over the years."

Arnie's mouth dropped open, and his eyes grew wide. "Really? Are you sure? I don't want to force you to do this and have you hate me for it in the future."

She smiled and moved closer to her husband, giving him a sweet kiss. "I'm sure. I want you to have your business."

"Whoo hoo!" he yelled, then covered his mouth, afraid he'd woken the kids.

Edna laughed softly. "I'm glad it makes you that happy. But just don't grumble to me when customers complain about their room, the food, or any number of things, and everything is always breaking down at the lodge."

He pulled her into a hug. "I won't complain if you won't."

"Deal," she whispered. And they kissed to seal the deal.

Chapter Two

Today - December 21st

Cassandra Nichols stood in her office high above Los Angeles, talking into her phone, trying to calm her client down. The view from her windows was spectacular, especially at night when the city lights sparkled below her, but Cassie rarely noticed. She was always too busy putting out fires for one celebrity or another.

"Colleen, sweetie. It's okay. All you have to do is show up, have your picture taken on the red carpet, then sneak out. You don't even have to talk to reporters. In and out. It's that easy," Cassie told the movie star client. Colleen Culvers was the hottest young star in the movies these days, and Cassie was lucky to be her public relations manager. Unfortunately, Colleen was an introvert and hated doing any publicity. Most of the time, Cassie had to go with her to an event and practically hold her hand throughout it.

"No, dear. You really can do this without me," Cassie said. "Can your sister go with you? I'm sure she'd enjoy walking the carpet with you." Cassie walked toward her desk to sit down, but the beeping on her phone telling her she had another call stopped her. She sighed.

"No, Colleen. I'm not sighing about you. Believe me, if I could come with you tonight, I would. But I have an important meeting. What if I sent a car for you, and my assistant can be on the sidelines with you?"

The beeping from the other call was driving Cassie crazy. The phone calls just never stopped. Didn't anyone text anymore?

"Okay. Sounds good, dear. You're going to do great tonight. Talk to you later." Cassie hung up, and the other call did, also. She dropped into her leather desk chair, kicked off her heels, and heaved a big sigh. Now, all she had to do was talk her assistant into babysitting Colleen tonight.

Cassie buzzed the office phone, and her assistant, Marcie James, glided in. Marcie was tall and slender with long legs that her heels made even longer. Her light brown skin always seemed to glow, and her short, dark, curly hair bounced as she walked. She could easily have been a model, but she was also the most organized person Cassie had ever met.

"Colleen needs a babysitter again tonight," Cassie told Marcie. "Is there any chance you'd want to take care of her tonight?"

Marcie smiled, showing perfectly straight teeth. "Sure. I don't mind."

"Thanks so much," Cassie said. "Blake and I haven't been out together in weeks, and I'd hate to cancel on him again." She glanced down at the three-carat diamond on her left hand. She and Blake had been engaged for two years, but they'd both been too busy with their jobs to even think about planning a wedding.

"You two go out and enjoy yourselves for a change," Marcie

said. "I can take care of Colleen. I'll take the car service to pick her up and hold her hand all evening."

"You're a lifesaver," Cassie said. At that moment, her phone beeped, and she glanced at her iPhone. This wasn't one of her celebrity clients. With another sigh, Cassie touched the earbud that seemed permanently glued to her ear and answered. "Hi, Jen. How are you?"

"Hi, Cassie. I'm fine. I hope I'm not bothering you," Jen said, sounding nervous.

"Of course not. I always have time for my best friend and favorite lodge manager," Cassie said, smiling to herself. Talking to Jennifer Taylor always brought back memories of grade school lunches and high school dances in Big Bear. They'd known each other since kindergarten, and now Jen was the manager of her family's lodge. "What can I do for you?"

"Well," Jen hesitated, then continued. "We have a problem here. Three more of our staff have quit and gone to other places in town to work. We're running the lodge on a shoestring and were packed with guests until New Year's Day."

Cassie frowned and began twirling a strand of her blond hair with her fingers. It was an old nervous habit that she'd never completely been able to break even at the age of thirty-two. "Why is everyone quitting? I offered to pay them more to stay on until the new year."

"I know," Jen said. "But there are job openings at all the hotels and resorts right now because they're all understaffed too, and since we're closing after New Year's, well, they don't want to risk not having a job next year."

Cassie understood their reasoning, but it didn't help her. She'd be glad when the lodge was no longer her problem after the first of the year. She had enough to worry about with her clients always calling her. "Jen, I don't know what I can do to help you. You'll just have to make do with the staff we have left."

"We could really use some help, Cassie. We're all going crazy here. Even Gabe has been pitching in wherever he can, but he's swamped as it is keeping up with repairs and driving guests around."

Cassie sighed again. Sighing seemed the only way for her to let go of her stress. Gabe. She was sure he was ready to blow up having to help around the lodge and do his handyman job, too. She understood it wasn't easy to keep the place running smoothly, especially now that he was the only one who could fix anything around there. But it was only for a few more weeks.

"Cass? Are you still there?" Jen asked.

"Yes. I'm here. I don't know what I can do to help, Jen. As much as I'd like to," Cassie said. Her phone was beeping in her ear and driving her crazy. It was one of her clients, and she should answer it, but she hated to leave Jen in a lurch.

"Can you come and help until Christmas?" Jen asked. "Or until after New Year's? I know you have a high-pressure job, but we really need the help. All our regulars are used to good service, and I don't know how we can give it to them with so little staff."

Cassie sat up in her chair. Come help at the lodge? How on earth did Jen think she could get away during the holidays? That's when her clients needed her the most. "I can't Jen. I'm sorry. I can't drop everything here and hop a plane to Big Bear. My clients are so demanding."

"Don't you get vacation time?" Jen asked. "Don't your clients ever go away for Christmas? It seems like you should at least be able to take a week off for the holidays."

Mountain View Lodge in Big Bear. Cassie thought about it for a moment. She grew up working there, even as a small child. First, her grandparents had owned it, then her parents. She remembered beautiful snowy Christmases with the lodge decorated and lit up charmingly. Every room in the lodge had a Christmas tree and garland around the fireplace. The staircase was covered in garland and lights, and red, gold, silver, and blue decorations covered every surface. It was an amazing place to have grown up in. But now that both of her parents had passed on, Cassie couldn't imagine it would feel the same. Still.

"Have the decorators been there?" Cassie asked Jen.

"Yes. Everything is beautiful. Our customers have all commented on how lovely it looks."

That incessant beeping in her ear was driving Cassie crazy. "Can I get back to you later this evening?" she asked Jen.

"Okay. But please think about coming to help. We need someone who knows this place inside-out."

"I'll let you know. Thanks, Jen. Hold down the fort until I call." They hung up, and Cassie waited another moment before answering the call that had been annoying her. "Hi, RD. Yeah, I've been on the phone. So sorry. What can I do for you?" Cassie stared at her watch as the young TikTok sensation turned pop star told her his newest press problem. Big Bear was sounding pretty good about now.

* * *

Later that evening, Cassie and Blake Chandler were seated in a private booth in their favorite upscale restaurant. They both had their earbuds in, as they always did, just in case a call came in. Blake was the manager of a wildly popular up-and-coming rock band, and it seemed the four guys could never do anything without calling him first. But then, Cassie was always on calls with her clients, too. Luckily, they both understood the pressure of working with celebrities, and neither expected the other to not be on call 24/7.

"How was your day?" Blake asked Cassie after they'd ordered and their wine had come.

Cassie looked up into Blake's deep blue eyes and smiled. Looking at his gorgeous face with the square jawline, deep-set eyes, and thick, sandy-blond hair always made her happy. They'd known each other for four years and had been living together for two, but she never tired of seeing him. She figured it was probably because they saw so little of each other with their busy schedules and his traveling with the band.

"It was the same as always," she answered. "Colleen was freaking out about her appearance tonight, and RD has a nude picture he says he sent to his girlfriend a year ago before becoming famous being spread around social media. You know, same old, same old." She grinned.

"Goodness. Your clients need to grow up," Blake said, moving closer to her. "But then, mine aren't any better. They fight over who gets to drink from which coffee mug when we travel on the bus. Really? Does it matter?"

Cassie laughed.

Blake leaned over and kissed her lightly on the lips. "I like hearing you laugh."

This made her smile. Blake was a romantic, and she loved that part of him. He could also be a bit snobbish and a little too conceited about how he looked and dressed, but she didn't mind. He was good about paying attention to her when they were together.

After their food arrived, Cassie brought up the subject she'd been thinking about all night. "The lodge is having staffing problems. Jen called me today and asked if I'd consider coming there over the holidays and helping."

Blake's perfectly shaped brows rose. "Really? What do they want you to do? Change sheets and clean toilets?"

His words stung. "If that's what needs to be done, maybe," Cassie said, harsher than she'd meant to. "But mostly, I'd work the desk and manage everything. Pretty much what my mother would be doing if she were still alive."

"Oh." Blake took a bite of his steak and chewed slowly before washing it down with a sip of wine. "Do you want to go there to help?"

"No. Not really," Cassie said. "But I don't think I have a choice. Christmas is our busiest time of year at the lodge. Even though we're going to close after New Year's, we need the income numbers to look good in case we can find a buyer."

"Hm. I see your point. But can you leave work over the holidays?" Blake asked.

Cassie sighed. "I can take calls from my clients in Big Bear just as easily as here, I guess. And many of them usually leave for the holidays, so there isn't as much going on. So, I suppose I can leave."

Blake leaned in closer to her. "What about our Christmas?" he asked huskily.

Cassie almost melted right there. She usually couldn't resist him when he used that voice. "You could come to the lodge and spend Christmas with me," she said hopefully. "I'll be staying in my parents' house, and we'll have it all to ourselves. It might be romantic, with the snow, crackling fireplace, and the pine trees."

He smiled. "It might be. Okay. We can try for that. It's a short flight from L.A. I have to be with the guys for their concert on December 23rd, but then I could be in Big Bear the next day."

"I knew you'd understand," Cassie said, feeling relieved. "It's just for two weeks, and then I don't have to worry about that place anymore."

"I'll drink to that," Blake said, raising his wine glass. Cassie did the same, and they clinked glasses. "Let's go home before either of us gets a phone call."

"I'll drink to that, too," Cassie said, finishing the last of her wine.

* * *

The next evening, Cassie was on the last flight out of L.A. to Big Bear. Jen had been thrilled to hear she was coming and told her she'd personally air out her mother's house and put fresh sheets on the bed in the guest room. Cassie wasn't sure how she felt about staying at her old house without her mother there. It would be strange, and empty. Her mother, Amanda Nichols, had passed away in June, and occasionally, Cassie had twinges of guilt over not going home more often to see her over the past few years. But it had been her mother who'd encouraged her from an early age to leave Big Bear and go to college. For whatever reason, her mother hadn't wanted Cassie to be stuck running the lodge for the rest of her life. Cassie always wondered if her mother had regretted staying in the vacation town instead of going out on her own.

The flight was shorter than the time it took Cassie to get through security at LAX. In under thirty minutes, the plane landed in Big Bear's small airport, and the thirty passengers disembarked to collect their bags, skis, snowboards, and other belongings. Cassie had checked a large bag and also had a carry-on. She hadn't been sure what she'd need for the next two weeks and had overpacked.

"There you are!" Jen called to her as she hurried toward the baggage claim area.

Cassie smiled, genuinely happy to see her old friend. Jen looked almost like she had in high school, with her thick, brown hair cut at chin length and cute glasses framing her sparkling blue eyes. It was always hard for Cassie to believe that her bubbly friend was a wife and mother of two children under the age of five. She had more energy than Cassie had ever had. The two hugged, then finally pulled apart so as not to block the other travelers trying to get their bags.

"I'm so glad you're here," Jen said, nearly breathless. "We've been going crazy with so little staff. But you'll be able to fix everything."

"Well, I'm not sure about that, but I'll do what I can," Cassie said. She walked over to the carousel and was about to pull her bag off when a man stepped up beside her.

"I'll get that for you," he said, lifting the heavy bag easily off the turnstile.

"Thanks," Cassie said, turning to him. Their eyes met, and that's when she realized she was looking into a familiar pair of dark brown eyes. "Oh, Gabe. I didn't know you had come along with Jen too."

Gabriel Kessler set the bag down and stared at her. "I always come along to pick up guests," he said sharply. "You know that."

Cassie bit her lip nervously, then made herself stop. She'd

known Gabe her entire life. They'd both lived at the lodge growing up, went to school together, and even worked alongside each other. He was the same age as her older brother, Jake, and they were practically like brother and sister. Well, practically, but not really. There had been that summer before senior year, but she didn't want to even think about that now. What she did know was that she wouldn't let Gabe intimidate her with his gruff attitude.

Jen linked arms with Cassie. "Let's get back to the lodge," she said, leading Cassie toward the parking lot. "At least everyone is checked in for the night, and the kitchen is finally closed. You and I can catch up while I help you unpack."

From behind her, Cassie felt Gabe's eyes boring into her as he followed with her suitcase. The wheels clacked along on the tile floor and then made an even louder thumping noise over the door jamb while leaving the airport. They reached the shuttle bus the lodge used to take guests to and from the airport or ski resorts in the area. Cassie climbed up on the bench seat next to Jen while Gabe lifted her suitcase into the back end.

"Sheesh. What did you pack in this bag? Rocks?" Gabe asked before slamming the shuttle bus's back door. He walked around to the driver's side and slid in behind the wheel.

"Yes, I packed rocks," Cassie said. "I figured there weren't enough rocks around here and thought I'd bring some."

Gabe twisted in his seat and eyed her, then his lips curled slightly into a smile. At least Cassie thought he smiled. His full dark beard and mustache did a pretty good job of hiding his lips.

Jen began chatting about what was happening at the lodge as they drove the short distance there. Cassie knew when her grandparents bought the lodge decades ago, it had seemed like the place was far out of town. But through the years, so much had grown up around it. Now, it was a quick trip from the airport to there.

As they pulled into the driveway, Cassie smiled. The lodge was lit up inside, giving it a warm glow through the large windows against the night sky. Christmas lights lit up the outside, too, framing the peaked roof at the entrance and the other peak over the large gathering room window. Twinkle lights had been placed around the trees in the yard as well, and the infinity pool on the left side of the lodge sparkled. The blanket of white snow seemed to glow under the moonlight. "Wow. It's so beautiful," Cassie said without thinking.

"You haven't been here for Christmas in a long time," Gabe said gruffly, breaking the mood.

Cassie frowned at him, but Jen spoke up quickly.

"The decorators did an amazing job this year, don't you think?" Jen nudged Cassie.

Cassie turned and smiled at her. "Yes, they did." She remembered when her grandmother and mother had decorated the lodge inside and out. It had been a big job. As the building grew bigger, they decided they could afford to have decorators come each year. It had been a big relief for her mother, who already worked too hard.

Gabe pulled around the lodge and followed the paved road toward the back of the property where Cassie's parents' house stood. The house sat among the tall pines, dark as the night sky. No decorations, no welcoming lights.

"You said not to bother to decorate the house," Jen said apologetically.

"I didn't think I'd be here," Cassie said. Now, she wished she'd had them at least trim the house with lights.

Gabe parked in front and got out to grab Cassie's bag from the back end. Before she left the van, Cassie's phone went off. She sighed and touched the earbud.

"Cassie here," she said. "Oh, hi, Colleen. Yes, I am out of town right now. Well, I was needed elsewhere. Is something wrong?"

Jen had left the car and headed inside to give Cassie privacy, but Gabe continued to stand by Cassie's door with his hand on her suitcase handle.

"Okay, Colleen. Everything will be fine. Just have your assistant block the guy from your Instagram account and delete the nasty comments. It's really as simple as that."

Gabe took in a big breath and let it out loudly.

"Colleen, I'm sure your assistant won't mind you asking her to do that. I don't have access to your account, so I can't delete it. Just call her and have her take care of it," Cassie said. She glanced over at Gabe and saw the disgusted look on his face. "Just go," she whispered to him, waving him away as she slipped out of the van. "I'll carry my own bag."

Gabe remained there, crossing his arms.

"No, Colleen. I wasn't saying that to you. Listen, I'll call your assistant and tell her to delete the comments, okay? You get some rest, and I'll talk to you tomorrow." Cassie tapped her earbud and sighed.

"Whose kid was that?" Gabe asked.

She glared at him. "It wasn't a kid. She's one of my clients. She's having a bad night."

"Who are you, her psychiatrist?" Gabe said. "Can't she delete her own Instabook comments?"

"It's not Instabook, it's Instagram," Cassie told him. She reached for her bag's handle, but Gabe held on firmly. "She's delicate. Most celebrities are. Give me my bag."

"I'll take it in for you," Gabe insisted. "That's my job."

She got ahold of the handle and pulled, but Gabe held on tight. They struggled with the bag for a moment, staring angrily at each other. Finally, Gabe gave it a hard tug, which made Cassie almost fall face-first into the snow.

"Cripes, Gabe. What's wrong with you?" Cassie yelled. "Why are you being such a jerk?"

Gabe glared at her. "I'm doing my job—while I still have one."

Cassie was about to retort, but her phone beeped again. Gabe rolled his eyes.

"Fine, answer your phone and take your own bag into the house," he said. "Obviously, this place means nothing to you." Gabe stormed off to the van and drove off.

Cassie watched him drive away, her heart beating wildly from their fight over the suitcase. The phone continued to beep. Finally, she answered with a touch of her earbud.

"Hi, Colleen. Yes, I will call your assistant. Give me a few minutes." Cassie grabbed her bag and headed toward the door. Jen had turned on the lights, making the house look welcoming. It had been her grandparents' house and then her parents' house. She dreaded staying here, knowing her mother wouldn't be in the room next to hers.

"Yes, Colleen. I'm still here. Just go to bed and get a good night's sleep. I promise those nasty comments will be gone by morning." As Cassie hung up, she wished her problems would be gone in the morning as well.

Chapter Three

Christmas – 1966

Edna finished decorating the last of the Christmas cookies and dropped onto a kitchen stool. This was their second Christmas owning the Mountain View Lodge—the name Arnie had decided upon. The lodge had a perfect view of the Snow Summit ski trails, and he'd thought the name suited it. In the year and a half they'd owned the lodge, Edna was surprised at how busy it had become. Even though they had only six rooms to offer guests, people came. Last year, they were filled with hunters in the early winter season, but much to Edna's surprise, couples and families came to stay over Christmas to ski. This year, all six rooms were filled over Christmas again, so Edna planned a Christmas Eve celebration in the living area for all the families.

"Those cookies smell great," Arnie said, sneaking one off the counter. He'd been careful to stay on the rug runner so his snowy boots wouldn't dirty the kitchen floor. They were in their cottage, and Craig and Amanda were fast asleep in their beds.

"I'm sure the guests and kids will enjoy them tomorrow night," Edna said. She stood and started placing the cookies in a Tupperware. "I can't believe we've been busy over the holidays again. I never knew people liked to take their vacations at Christmastime to ski. We're booked through the New Year."

Arnie grinned. "Isn't that nice? When we bought this place, I wasn't sure we'd have guests after hunting season. But we've fixed the lodge up pretty nicely, so families like it here too."

Edna nodded. The first winter had been hard on her. She wasn't a fan of the cold or snow, and getting up early to cook meals for hunters wore her down. But when they'd booked the entire holiday season that year, she'd been surprised. It was still hard work, but she enjoyed the families that came for the holidays, and many of the same ones came again this year.

"It's going to be even busier when we add on the addition with four more rooms behind the lodge next summer," Arnie said. "But I'm excited about it. We've done so much better than I thought for our first year and a half. Maybe we'll be able to add on a little each year."

"Then you'd better put some money aside so we can hire help to clean rooms and cook," Edna said. "Because I can barely keep up as it is."

Arnie drew closer and placed a kiss on his wife's lips. "If we expand, we'll get help, too. I may even need someone to help me around the place. Driving guests to and from the ski resorts, keeping everything running smoothly, and bringing in wood for the fireplace is getting to be a lot of work. But I'm happy we're doing so well." Arnie had bought an old '57 Chevy panel truck that held six people so he could take guests to and from the ski resorts. He hadn't thought he'd need one so quickly but was happy they were busy all year round.

Edna placed the last of the cookies in a container and snapped on the lid. "I have to admit, I didn't think we'd do this well for a while. But I'm glad we are." She smiled. "And I'm glad you're doing something you enjoy."

"Me too, sweetheart. I know you work hard around here, but someday, we'll make enough so we can hire help, and all you'll have to do is count the money." Arnie grinned mischievously.

Edna laughed. "Yeah, right."

Arnie went to the door and doffed his boots on the rug. "I can't do one more thing tonight." He went up next to Edna and wrapped his arms around her. "Let's go to bed."

Edna's brows rose. "I have an early day tomorrow."

He laughed. "I don't have the strength for any hanky panky. I meant, let's go to bed and sleep!"

Together, they shut off the kitchen light and walked down the hallway to their bedroom.

* * *

The next day was Christmas Eve, and the guests and their children were all in good spirits. The tree had been put up a few days earlier and twinkled with lights and mercury glass ornaments. Edna had run garland down the staircase railing and added lights there also. A beautiful wreath hung on the front door, and Arnie had trimmed the outside roof with lights. With a fresh blanket of snow on the ground, the lodge looked like a Christmas card photo.

The guests ate breakfast early and headed to the ski resorts. Some wanted to go into town for some last-minute shopping. All the guests were looking forward to a turkey dinner with all the trimmings and treats that evening at the lodge.

"It's so nice of you to put on a celebration for all of us," Mrs. Janet Henley told Edna as she poured more coffee in her mug. "We just love staying here. It's so cozy and inviting."

"Thank you," Edna said. It felt nice when guests appreciated the extra things they did. "We want people to feel at home here."

"Well, you're doing a great job of it," Albert Henley said. "And the boys love it here, too. We live here in California on the coast, so they only see snow when we come here."

Edna smiled over at the couple's boys, George and Harry. They were typical boys at ages five and seven—full of energy and busy all the time. Her son, Craig, now age six, had fun playing with the kids who came to the lodge, especially boys his age.

Other guests told Edna they were excited for the holiday celebration that night before leaving to ski or shop. Edna hoped they wouldn't be disappointed. All she'd planned to do was have dinner, then offer cookies and cider in the living area while they played Christmas music on the record player. She'd also bought a few little toys and wrapped them for the children staying at the resort.

"How's the turkey coming along?" Arnie asked a few hours later as he entered the lodge's kitchen from the back door. He'd been shoveling the fresh snow off the walking paths and driveway in-between driving guests from place to place.

"It's right on time," Edna said. After washing the dishes from breakfast, she'd prepared the turkey and placed it in the gas oven. While it cooked, she'd had little Amanda, now four, follow her around upstairs to clean rooms for the guests and, as always, tried to make it feel like a game. Edna had worn the little girl out enough for her to take a nap on the little cot inside the pantry.

"Great. I can't wait," Arnie said, grinning. "I'll bring in more firewood for the fireplace, and yes, I'll mop the floor afterward so you won't have to. The radio says we have a windstorm coming tonight, and I don't want to bring in wood during that." He shivered.

"Brr. I don't blame you," Edna said. She was so tired already, and they had a whole evening of entertaining to do. "Have you seen where Craig is? He left the kitchen to look for you earlier."

"He's out building a snowman with the Henley boys. They came back a little while ago from skiing."

"Good. It's so hard to get all this work done and keep an eye on the kids. I'm glad Amanda still takes naps," Edna said.

Evening fell early, with the sky turning dark around 4:30. Dinner was set for six. Arnie had brought all the guests back to the lodge earlier and had showered and changed. As he served drinks to the guests in the living area, little Amanda played dolls with the daughter of another guest, and Craig was busy playing a game with George. Everyone was tired and hungry and ready to eat their holiday meal.

Suddenly, all the lights went out!

Arnie waited a moment for his eyes to adjust to the dim light. Luckily, the light from the blazing fireplace allowed them to see a little. "Don't worry, everyone," Arnie told the guests. "The wind must have blown a line down. I'll get some candles and oil lamps, and we'll be just fine."

"I'll help you." Albert Henley stood and followed Arnie into the kitchen, where they kept the candles in the pantry. Edna had already lit a couple of candles and placed them on the counters so she could see.

"I'll set candles in the dining room and living room so you

can keep working on dinner," Arnie told Edna.

But Edna looked at him, exasperated. "How am I supposed to finish dinner without electricity?"

"The stove is gas. It'll keep running. What else do you need?"

Edna sighed. "Never mind. I'll figure it out myself."

Janet Henley came into the kitchen. "What can I do to help?" she asked, grabbing an apron from the hooks by the door and already tying it on.

"Oh, thank goodness." Edna looked relieved. "Thank you so much! The potatoes need mashing, and I need to get the turkey out of the oven and make gravy. Can you stir the vegetables that are on the stove, too?"

Janet smiled. "Sure thing."

The men set up candles and oil lamps on safe surfaces and on each of the dining room tables. Soon, both rooms were aglow with light.

"This is better than electricity," Albert told Arnie. "It's like an old-fashioned Christmas."

Arnie chuckled. "Don't tell Edna that. I'm sure no electricity is making it harder to finish the dinner."

Despite the lack of electricity, Edna and Janet did finish making dinner and set the food on the side tables, buffet-style. Then everyone sat down and had a nice candlelit meal.

"This is fun!" George said, stuffing more turkey and cranberry sauce into his mouth.

"It's like the olden days," Craig said gleefully.

The adults laughed, many of them having lived in the "olden days."

Arnie had found a battery-powered radio and turned it on. Luckily, a radio station playing Christmas music came through.

"Well, someone has power out there," he said.

"Hopefully, we will soon, too," Edna said softly to him at their table. "But everyone seems to be enjoying the novelty of no lights."

Arnie reached over and squeezed her hand. "The meal is delicious, and the candlelight is fun for a change. We couldn't have planned a better Christmas Eve."

After everyone had eaten until they were as stuffed as the turkey, they all sat in the living room near the tree. Arnie brought in the radio, and he and Edna served warm cider in heavy mugs to the guests. Some of the adults chose to add a little vodka to their cider for a merrier holiday.

In all, there were fourteen adults and eleven children. The tree lights weren't working, but the glass ornaments sparkled in the firelight and candlelight. Edna passed out cookies to everyone who had room to eat them and then settled in on the upright piano bench and began to play Silver Bells. Soon, all the adults and some of the children were singing along to the holiday songs she played. Halfway through a rowdy rendition of Rudolph the Red-Nosed Reindeer, the lights came on, startling everyone.

"Aww," some of the children proclaimed sorrowfully. They'd been having so much fun with the lights out. Even the adults seemed disappointed that the electricity had come on.

"I can fix this," Arnie said. He walked around the room, turning off the lights. Everyone cheered. Then Edna started playing Rudolph again, and the kids sang along.

Later that evening, after the dishes had been washed and their kids were tucked away in bed, Arnie and Edna lay cuddled up in bed.

"It was a great Christmas Eve," Arnie said, squeezing her

affectionately. "Probably the best we've ever had."

"Memorable," Edna said softly. "It's something the kids will remember for years to come."

"It's fun having guests here for Christmas, isn't it?" Arnie asked. "It's like having one big happy family."

"It is. Even though I'd like my parents to come for the holidays, the guests make up for it," she said.

"I wish your parents could come, too. But I'm afraid they don't want to drive this far. Maybe someday we can arrange for them to come and stay."

"Maybe," Edna said. "But until then, our guests make the holidays fun."

"It will get better every year," Arnie said. "Maybe our guests will come year after year and actually be like family. I'm looking forward to the future here."

"Me, too," Edna said.

He kissed her lightly on the lips. "Merry Christmas, dear."

"Merry Christmas."

They fell asleep in each other arms, feeling satisfied with the warm, loving home and friends they'd made in the short time they'd lived in Big Bear.

Chapter Four

Today - December 23ʳᵈ

Cassie woke up early the next day, ready to work at the lodge. She bundled up in a thick coat and boots to walk the short distance from her parents' house to the main lodge. It had snowed overnight, and a fresh layer of white powder covered the walkways. The air was crisp, and despite having lived in the warmer climate of L.A. these past few years, Cassie actually enjoyed the cold, clean air.

As she walked, Cassie thought about what Gabe had said angrily to her last night. *This place means nothing to you!* Those words had haunted her all night. He was wrong. She'd grown up at the lodge and worked there until she left for college. She loved the place for its history. Cassie loved hearing stories about the early days when her grandparents had owned it and had listened intently when her mother or father told stories of their first years running the place. If her mother hadn't insisted she go to college, Cassie might have actually stayed and taken the lodge over. But her mother hadn't wanted Cassie to give up college for the lodge. Even when her father died in a car accident during her first year of college, her mother had refused to let her stay at the lodge and help.

"You need your own life, away from here," her mother had told her. So, Cassie had done that. She'd finished school, majoring in public relations and communications, and had worked her way up in one of the most successful public relations firms in L.A. But even after all she'd accomplished, it didn't mean that Cassie didn't care about her family's legacy—the Mountain View Lodge.

As Cassie drew closer to the lodge's back door, she saw Gabe shoveling snow off the walkways. She'd have a talk with him later to find out why he was so angry at her. Obviously, he didn't want her to sell the lodge, but she had no choice. Couldn't he see that? With a sigh, Cassie entered the building.

The lodge had changed significantly since the days when her grandparents opened it. There'd been a devastating fire in 1970, and it had been completely rebuilt. And through the years, many new additions had been added on. They now had sixty rooms of varying sizes, a spa where guests could enjoy a massage, skin treatments, saunas, and other treatments, a work-out room, an indoor pool, and an outdoor pool for the summer. The main lodge had a dining room where they served a complimentary breakfast, a bar in the living area where guests could have drinks in the evenings only, and the lovely living area where the original stone fireplace still stood with a welcoming crackling fire.

Yes, the place had changed a lot, but as the years passed, the same guests still came to enjoy the homestyle feel of the warm wooden lodge and the high-end accommodations.

"Ah, there you are," Jen said, happy to see Cassie. "I'll let you take over the desk, and I'll go help in the dining room and kitchen." Jen rushed off from behind the desk that sat between the living area and the dining room.

"Okay," Cassie said to Jen's retreating back. It had been a while since she'd worked at the front desk. She hoped she remembered what to do. Soon, guests came to the desk to ask about a ride downtown, extra towels, or to check out, and Cassie fell back easily into the routine.

An hour went by quickly, and during a lull, Cassie watched as Gabe strode toward the desk. He still looked angry, although she still didn't understand why. But she also couldn't help but notice how well he'd kept himself in shape after all these years and how good his jeans looked on him. *Sheesh. Get a grip!* she thought.

"Does anyone need a ride yet?" Gabe asked, crossing his arms over his chest. All the workers wore white cotton dress shirts with the company name embroidered on them, along with dark slacks or skirts. But not Gabe. He wore a long-sleeved black T-shirt with a red-plaid flannel shirt over it. In a way, it was his uniform. As long as she could remember, Gabe wore flannel shirts winter and summer.

"Yes," Cassie answered, looking at her notes. "Two couples need a ride to town at nine. Then a group of five people need a lift to the ski resort at nine-thirty."

"Okay. I'll get the shuttle bus and will be waiting outside the front door."

"Great," Cassie said, choosing to ignore his grumpy attitude. Just then, her earbuds buzzed, and she glanced at her phone and sighed.

"Another one of your childish celebrities?" Gabe asked, looking smug.

Cassie sneered at him and turned around, answering the

phone. "Hi, Joe. How's everything going?" Joe Keagan was a twenty-one-year-old basketball player who'd left college when he was drafted by the NBA. He also was always getting into trouble because he hung out in bars and gambled too much in Las Vegas.

"Listen, Joe. You need to stay away from Vegas. You're going to spend all your money before you even earn it. And you know you always get in fights when you drink too much. I'll call Ceasar's to see if I can smooth things over, okay? But please, no more fighting." Cassie tapped the earbud and spun around. Her heart jumped when she saw Gabe still standing there, staring at her.

"Sheesh! I thought you'd left by now," Cassie said, placing a hand over her heart. "Snoop much?"

Gabe broke out with laughter. "Snoop much? Does anyone even talk like that anymore?"

This really flustered Cassie. "Don't you have to get the shuttle bus?" she asked tersely. The lodge telephone rang, and she scooped it up to answer. "Mountain View Lodge. This is Cassie." She heard Gabe chuckle again as he walked away. He was so frustrating!

Later, after the dining room was closed, Jen came out to the desk for a moment. "How is everything going?" she asked.

"Fine. I was afraid I'd forgotten how to run the desk, but it all came back to me," Cassie said. "What do you need me to do now?"

Jen chuckled. "You're the owner, and I'm just the manager. I think I should be asking you that question."

Cassie laughed. "Yeah, but I haven't been working here in a long time. And you run the place now. So tell me where I'm needed the most."

"You can stay at the desk. I'll go help the maids clean the rooms. We're short two maids today."

Cassie considered Jen a moment. Her friend was young, but she probably had her fill of changing sheets and cleaning bathrooms at home with her two kids. "I can go help the maids," Cassie offered. "Remember, I used to clean rooms for my parents. That's how I started out here."

Jen looked horrified. "I can't let you do that. Sometimes, it's a really nasty job."

"Oh, please," Cassie told her. "There's nothing I've never seen before."

An hour later, Cassie had changed the beds in two rooms, vacuumed, and cleaned bathrooms. But at the moment, she was staring at the grossest mess she'd ever seen. A guest had clogged the toilet, let it overflow, and hadn't bothered to tell the front desk. "I think I'm going to be sick," Cassie said to herself.

Holding her breath, Cassie grabbed the plunger from her cart and tried plunging the toilet. Water was overflowing onto the floor, and it wasn't clean water. She gagged.

"What the hell?" a male voice said behind her.

Cassie turned, and there stood Gabe, looking as horrified as she felt.

"It was like this when I got here," Cassie told him. "But the more I plunge, the more water spills out. It's so disgusting."

"Go get a mop and a clean bucket of water, and I'll get a snake. I don't think plunging is going to fix this problem," Gabe said, leaving the room. Cassie was all too happy to leave the disgusting bathroom and find a pail and mop on her cart.

By the time Gabe had returned from the janitor's closet, Cassie had mopped up most of the dirty water from the bathroom floor. Gabe ran the snake down the toilet, and soon the water began going down. Finally, he flushed it, and they both held their breath, hoping the water would go down and not rise up again.

"There," Gabe said. "It's working now. Next time, ask me to help. That was a gross mess you had there."

"Hey! I hope you mean it was a gross mess a guest left behind, not my mess," Cassie said.

Gabe chuckled. "I know it's from the guest. Don't take offense."

Standing in the small bathroom together, her holding a mop and him holding the snake, they both laughed.

"Just like old times," Gabe said, his voice tender instead of angry. "Remember when we were teens? Back then, I was fixing stuff in the lodge, and you were cleaning rooms."

"Yeah. Nothing's changed, I guess," Cassie said.

The smile faded from Gabe's face. "But it will change, and soon. This place will be closed soon."

Cassie didn't want to see angry Gabe return. "I'm hoping it'll sell soon, and then everyone will still have a job. This is a nice resort, and customers love it. I'm sure a new owner could do well here."

Gabe frowned but didn't give her a nasty retort. "More than likely, some hotel conglomerate will buy it and want to staff it with their own people," he said. "There won't be room for a handyman like me. They'll probably even tear down the caretaker's cottage I live in."

Cassie wanted to say that wasn't true, but she didn't know for sure. If a large company wanted to buy the lodge, she couldn't afford to say no. But it made her sad to think they'd destroy everything around there that made it so special. "Let's hope not," she said softly.

Gabe suddenly looked uncomfortable. "Well, I'd better get back to work. Good luck with the cleaning."

This made Cassie smile, but Gabe strode out as quickly as he'd appeared. With a sigh, Cassie finished cleaning the room and headed to the next one.

Later that evening, Cassie made herself a quick sandwich in the kitchen and sat alone in the dining room with most of the lights off. She could have gone back to the house to eat, but she preferred eating here. Jen had left for the night, and a young man named Jared was working the front desk overnight.

Cassie was tired. It had been a long day, and she could barely move. Every muscle ached. She hadn't worked this hard physically in a long time. Most of her work took a toll on her mentally. She took spin classes and Pilates, but they hadn't prepared her for cleaning rooms all day. That was work!

"Hey, there, Cassie. Remember me?" An older gentleman stepped inside the dining room and smiled at her.

"Mr. Henley! Of course, I remember you," Cassie said, standing up and hugging him. "How could I forget our favorite holiday guest."

He grinned. "Now, just call me George, okay? You're all grown up, and there's no sense in calling me Mr. anymore."

"Okay. George. Where's your wife? And are your kids here, too?"

George chuckled. "Yes. We're all here, and the grandchildren too. When we heard it was your last year owning the lodge, we all had to come. It'll be sad to see the place sell to someone else."

Cassie nodded. She'd heard that from so many returning guests today. "Come sit down and tell me how everyone is."

George followed her to the table and sat across from her. He was a tall man with a head of thick silver hair. Cassie figured he was around sixty-two years old because he and his wife had been close in age to her parents' ages.

"Becky and I are doing well, and the kids and grandkids are too," George said. "Of course, Becky and I no longer ski—we don't need any broken bones—but the kids have been out skiing and enjoying the nice weather."

"I'm glad," Cassie said.

"Say. I'm sorry to hear that your mother passed away last June. We heard too late that she had, and missed the funeral. She was such a nice woman and a heck of a good cook. Both of your parents were good friends to me and the wife. They are greatly missed around here," George said.

"Thank you," Cassie said. "I miss them a lot. This place isn't the same without them."

George gave her a small smile. "You know, my parents brought us boys here for the first time back in 1966. Your grandparents had just opened the place the year before, and we were one of the first families to start coming here for Christmas."

Cassie smiled. She knew this, but she let the older man reminisce. "It was a lot different back then, though, wasn't it? I remember my grandfather saying they had only six rooms and two bathrooms when they started the place. And the caretaker's house was their family house then."

"That's the truth. Why, I could tell you so many stories. Your Uncle Craig and I used to get up to mischief back then, and when she got older, your mother joined right in. I have a great many memories," George said, his eyes dreamy.

Cassie leaned forward in her chair. "Tell me some."

He laughed. "Well, the first one that comes to mind is the

very first Christmas we spent here. The place was full, so there were several adults and children running around. I was about five years old then. Your grandparents had put a tall tree up in the corner by the stone fireplace and decorated it, and there were lights and decorations all around. Your grandmother made a big turkey dinner with all the delicious side dishes. And right before we were supposed to eat, the power went out, and we were all sitting in the dark."

Cassie's brows shot up. She'd never heard this story before. "What did you all do? Was Grandma able to finish making the dinner?"

"Oh, yes. Luckily, she had a gas stove that was powered by propane. My mother helped her finish making dinner while my father and your grandfather lit candles and oil lamps and placed them all around. My dear, it was magical."

"It sounds magical," Cassie said, trying to imagine the old lodge and all of them eating by candlelight. It sounded cozy and delightful.

"And you know what?" George continued. "We enjoyed it so much that when the lights came on after dinner while we were all sitting around the piano singing Christmas carols, your grandfather turned the lights off. Everyone cheered, and we continued singing by candlelight."

Cassie laughed. It sounded like something her grandfather would have done. "That sounds like a wonderful Christmas."

"It was. And your grandmother had bought small gifts for each of the kids to open that night. I got a little Matchbox Car, and I loved it. It was a blue truck, and I kept it on my dresser for years. That was one of my most memorable Christmases ever."

"I love hearing stories like that," Cassie told him. She'd

heard many throughout the years, but this one warmed her heart. "Thanks for sharing it with me."

George smiled warmly. "After fifty-seven years of coming here for the Christmas holidays, I have plenty of memories. A lot has changed, but the warmth your family has always given to their guests has never changed. I'll be sorry to see it end."

Cassie suddenly felt sad. "I'll be sorry too, but I can't keep the resort anymore. It's grown so much, it takes a lot of time to run it, and I have a career and life in L.A."

George stood. "I know, dear. And you've made a good life for yourself, from what your mother had told me. Well, I hadn't meant to take up so much of your time. If you want to hear any more stories, let me know. My memory is full of them."

"I'd love to hear them all while you're here," Cassie said. As she watched him leave the room, she realized this would be her last chance to hear any of the old stories about the lodge, and that broke her heart.

She finished eating and said goodnight to Jared at the front desk. It had been a long day, and she was ready to drop into bed. Bundling up in her coat and boots, Cassie began walking toward the back of the property to her parents' house.

"I'm going to have to stop referring to it as my parents' house," she said to herself as she walked. Technically, it was her house now. But it seemed so strange.

As she rounded the corner of the driveway, Cassie gasped. Her house was trimmed with twinkle lights, and more lights covered bushes and trees in the yard. She smiled wide. Jen must have asked someone to decorate the house after all.

Picking up her pace, Cassie entered through the front door. The lights were on inside. "Who's here?" she called.

"It's just me," a male voice called back.

As Cassie entered the living room, she was stunned to see Gabe standing on a stepstool, hanging Christmas lights on a tall spruce tree. "You?" she asked.

"Yep. Me." Gabe stepped down from the stool. "It's Christmas Eve tomorrow. I figured you needed a Christmas tree."

Tears filled Cassie's eyes. This was the last thing she'd expected, and his thoughtfulness touched her heart. Gabe, the grumpy elf, had wanted to make her Christmas cheerier.

"Hey." Gabe came up to her, looking concerned. "Why the tears? I thought this would make you happy."

She swiped at the tears falling down her cheeks. "It has made me happy. Happier than you'd ever know. It's just so unexpected."

Gabe pulled her into a hug. "You had a hard day. I just wanted to make it better for you."

Cassie hugged him close. His aftershave tickled her nose, and she inhaled the woodsy scent. It suited him.

Gabe finally pulled away and looked at her. "All better?"

She nodded.

"Good. Because we need to get up in the attic and find some tree decorations," Gabe said. "Are you up to it?"

"Definitely," Cassie said excitedly.

Not only did they find a large box of old mercury glass ornaments, but Cassie brought out a bottle of Chardonnay and two glasses from the kitchen.

"Wine and tree decorating go together well," she said, smiling.

Gabe snorted. "I won't disagree, but we'd better be careful not to break these old ornaments."

They carefully unpacked the ornaments and started hanging them on the tree. Cassie knew that many of the ornaments had belonged to her grandmother and may have even hung on the tree in the old lodge in 1966.

"George Henley told me a cute story about the lodge and my grandparents the second year it was open. It always amazes me how long this place has been in business," Cassie said, sipping her wine and perusing the boxes of decorations.

"Me, too," Gabe said, hanging the smaller ornaments up near the top of the tall tree. "My dad started working here when your grandparents owned it, long before he married. Then, when he married my mom, your grandparents paid to have the cottage moved to where it is now so my dad and mom could live there and have a little privacy.

"I suppose after they built this house, they didn't need it anymore," Cassie said. "It was nice of them to let your family live there all these years."

Gabe nodded. "It's the only home I've ever known."

Cassie's heart clenched. She hadn't thought about that when she decided to sell the place. Gabe would have to leave if he wasn't asked to stay, and maybe even if he was, the new owners might want to use the cottage for other purposes. Not wanting to go there yet with Gabe and start a fight, she asked, "How is your father doing?"

Gabe took a deep breath and sat down on the sofa. "He's been declining pretty quickly. I kept him home with me as long as I could, but for his safety, he had to move into an assisted living unit. Now, the doctors tell me he may need around-the-clock care in a nursing facility."

Cassie sat down beside him. "I'm so sorry, Gabe. I had no idea Mitch was doing so badly."

Gabe nodded. "I was told his Parkinson's Disease would progress gradually, but it affected him quicker than most. And he's also experiencing memory loss. He's confused now when I visit him and sometimes doesn't even know who I am."

Cassie shook her head sadly. She'd always liked Mitch. He'd worked as the lodge's caretaker for her whole life, and it wasn't the same without him around. When his wife died of cancer when Gabe was five years old, her mother had looked after Gabe like he was her own child. She, Gabe, and her older brother Jake had played together as children, then worked at the lodge as teens. It saddened her to think of Mitch doing so poorly.

"I really am sorry, Gabe," Cassie said. "Is there anything I can do to help?"

Gabe turned and gazed into her eyes. "Don't sell the lodge?" he said.

Cassie sighed and ran a hand through her blond hair. "If only it were that easy. But I can't keep it and manage it from L.A. I hope whoever buys it will keep you and everyone else working here."

Gabe grinned mischievously. "Well, it was worth a try asking."

Cassie hit him playfully on the shoulder. "So you thought you could give me a sob story so I wouldn't sell?"

He turned serious again. "No. Everything I said was true. My father is doing badly. But life would be easier if this place didn't close down."

"I'm sorry," Cassie said again. And she really was. A part of her wanted to keep the lodge because it had been in her family for so long. But she'd lived in L.A. since college and had worked her way up in the PR firm. She couldn't see herself quitting her job or running the lodge from so far away.

They resumed decorating the tree, and the mood lightened again.

"By the way," Cassie said after feeling relaxed from a second glass of wine. "Why were you such a jerk to me when I arrived yesterday?"

"Was I?" he asked, then laughed. "I'm sorry. I know I was a jerk. I'd worked myself up so much over this place closing after New Year's Eve that by the time you arrived, I was mad as hell. I shouldn't have taken my frustrations out on you."

She shrugged. "I get it." After hanging a few more ornaments, she stopped and stared at Gabe. "Hey? Have you ever thought about buying the lodge? Or you and a few of the long-time employees could chip in together to buy it."

Gabe shook his head. "I don't have that kind of money, and I'm sure everyone else wouldn't have money to pool together to buy it either. I know what this place is worth, and it's way out of my range."

She nodded. "It was a thought."

"What about your brother, Jake?" Gabe asked. "Would he be interested in running the lodge?"

Cassie shook her head. "No. I asked him. He's content in Denver and loves his job as a pilot. He's looking forward to the money from the sale. He gets half when we sell."

"And if you don't sell?" Gabe asked.

"If by some miracle I wanted to keep running the lodge, he gets half the profits. Jake is fine with it either way. I just don't see how I could keep it."

The tree was finally finished, and Gabe threw another log into the fireplace. They packed up the box with empty decoration boxes, and then they both fell onto the sofa with the last of the wine.

"It's been a long day," Gabe said, glancing at the clock over the mantel. "And tomorrow will be busy. Christmas Eve—the annual dinner and celebration with the guests."

Cassie scrunched down on the sofa and laid her head back. "I've always loved the holiday celebrations at the lodge, but they're a lot of work. My mom worked hard every year, so I guess this year it's on me."

"There was no one better than your mom," Gabe said, smiling over at her.

"I totally agree," she said.

They sat quietly for a while, enjoying the warmth of the crackling fire and staring at the tree ornaments twinkling from the lights. Gabe turned and looked at Cassie, and she gazed up into his warm brown eyes.

"It's been a long time since we've spent time alone together," he said.

"It has," she said softly. As she looked at him, a warm feeling ran through her. She remembered when they'd been a couple years ago and how much in love she'd been with him. Gabe had always made her feel safe and loved. Suddenly, she wanted nothing more than to kiss him. As if reading her thoughts, Gabe leaned over and brushed his lips over hers.

They were jarred apart by the sound of her phone buzzing.

Cassie shook her head as if coming out of a fog and picked up her phone.

"Hello? Oh, hi, Blake. Yeah, I was still awake. We just finished decorating a tree here at the house." She stood and walked toward the fireplace, suddenly feeling she should put space between herself and Gabe.

Gabe stood and lifted the empty box of decorations, taking them upstairs.

"You can't come here for Christmas? Are you sure?" Cassie asked. She was used to Blake missing holidays, birthdays, and other special occasions. Work always came first.

"Do you think you could come for New Year's Eve? We always have a big party here at the lodge," Cassie told him. "Great. We'll plan for that. I'll miss you, too. Bye." Cassie set her phone down on the coffee table. When she turned around, she saw Gabe staring at her.

"Was that one of your spoiled clients?" he asked.

"No. It was Blake. He can't make it for Christmas," Cassie said. She suddenly felt uncomfortable talking about Blake with Gabe. They'd been seconds from kissing when the phone had interrupted them. Now, it felt like they were miles apart.

"Your boyfriend?" Gabe asked, shoving his hands in his jeans pockets.

Cassie hesitated before answering. "Actually, my fiancé."

Gabe's eyes immediately went to her ring finger. "You aren't wearing a ring," he said accusingly.

Cassie stared at her empty ring finger. "No, I'm not. I didn't think I should wear it while I was cleaning rooms. I didn't want to lose it." It wasn't the complete truth. Cassie had put it away before arriving at the lodge. She hadn't wanted to explain to everyone she'd been engaged for two years and hadn't yet planned a wedding.

Gabe cleared his throat. "Well, it's late. I'm going home. Goodnight." His words were stilted, and he sounded angry.

Before Cassie could respond, Gabe strode out of the house and was halfway to his truck.

Chapter Five

April 1970

Edna sighed as she finished cleaning the last of the guest rooms. It was April, and that meant they were closed for two weeks before the summer tourist season began. Edna and Arnie did this every year to give themselves a break from guests and to give the lodge a good cleaning.

In the years since they'd bought the lodge, Arnie had built two additions that held eight more rooms. They had also added small bathrooms to each room upstairs, so the guests no longer had to share. As they added on, the rooms filled up both summer and winter. They had many return customers and now thought of them as friends. After five years, their life in Big Bear was going quite well.

For Edna, it was easier now that both children were in school. She no longer had to keep an eye on the kids during the day while she cooked and cleaned. And in the summer, there were always other children around for the kids to play with and keep them busy.

"Next year, we're putting in a pool," Arnie announced

when Edna returned to the kitchen with her cleaning supplies.

"A pool! Are you crazy?" Edna laughed.

"Why not? We can build it right out back in the courtyard. It'll set us back a year from adding on more rooms, but the guests will love it," Arnie said.

Edna shook her head. "More than likely the bears will love it. What about building our new house?"

He grinned. "We'll get to that soon, too," he said. "But the cottage isn't all that bad, is it?"

"It's fine for now," Edna said. "But I'd really like a newer home with better insulation and a big fireplace to keep us warm."

"Someday soon," Arnie promised.

They went to bed that night in the cottage, relieved to have two weeks where they didn't have to rush around waiting on guests. Around three in the morning, Edna awoke to the smell of smoke. Thinking the fireplace was smoldering, she got up groggily, put on her robe and slippers, and walked toward the living room. The sight that greeted her out the living room window made her scream.

Arnie rushed to her, half-awake. "What is it?" he asked, looking around.

Edna was too stunned to speak. She pointed out the window. Arnie followed her arm, and his eyes grew wide. "Fire," he said in disbelief. Once reality hit him, he rushed to the phone to call the head of the volunteer fire department.

"Randy!" he said hurriedly once the man had answered. "It's Arnie at Mountain View Lodge. The lodge is on fire! Please come quickly."

Randy didn't even respond. He hung up, leading Arnie to believe he was on his way.

Edna had finally found her bearings. She rushed into the bedroom and quickly dressed in pants and a sweater and called for Arnie to get dressed, too. Then, they both put on their boots and coats at the door and headed out.

"What should we do?" Edna asked, terrified at the flickering flames in front of them.

Arnie looked around and saw the hose by the side of the house. It wasn't hooked up because nights were still cold, and it could freeze. He also looked at the trees around the lodge and how close the cottage now seemed to the fire. "Grab the hose and hook it up," he told Edna. "Spray down the front of the cottage so it won't catch fire. I'll see if I can get the lodge's hose to work and try to water down the lodge, too."

"Be careful," Edna yelled to Arnie as he ran off. She hurried to the hose and dragged it to the outdoor faucet. Her fingers fumbled, trying to screw it onto the faucet. It was cold out, and she was already shivering. She hoped the cold and the damp ground would keep the fire from coming to the house.

"Mom. What happened?" Ten-year-old Craig and eight-year-old Amanda stood on the front porch, staring at the fire.

"The lodge is on fire," Edna told them. "But we should be safe here at the house. Go inside and dress in warm clothes, just in case. I'll get you if I think we have to leave."

"But Mom," Craig said.

"Go inside!" she yelled. She was fearful that Craig would run off to help his father.

The kids did as they were told, and Edna finally got the hose working. She sprayed the front of the house until it was dripping wet, then sprayed the entire yard. Edna hoped it wouldn't freeze. As she sprayed the yard, she looked frantically for Arnie but didn't see him. The lodge's hose was hooked up near the back of the new addition, but she didn't see him anywhere.

"Be safe," she whispered as tears fell down her cheeks. She was watching their entire life burning down before her, and she couldn't bear to lose Arnie, too.

Finally, she heard the fire truck coming down the road and turning into the driveway. She couldn't see it or the men because of the lodge and the flames. She heard another truck, which she assumed was the water tanker. From her view, they were too late to save any of the buildings.

A few minutes later, Arnie came walking toward the house. Edna dropped the hose and ran to him. "You're okay," she said, relieved. In her mind, she'd thought she'd already lost him.

"I'm okay," he said tiredly, then opened his arms and hugged her close. "Randy told me to come back to the house to make sure you were okay."

"I'm okay," she said.

Still in each other's arms, they turned and looked at the lodge. It was completely engulfed by flames.

"Randy said it looks like a total loss, but they want to make sure the fire doesn't spread to the forest. They're spraying all around the lodge, but they can't save it," Arnie said. He looked at Edna, his eyes watery. "We've lost everything."

"Not everything," she said as tears filled her eyes.

Arnie nodded. "You're right. We have each other, the kids, and this house."

"We'll be okay," Edna said, trying to be brave.

Arnie nodded again, and they both watched as five years of hard work burned down before their eyes.

* * *

It took the rest of the night for the firefighters to put out the flames and proclaim the area safe. By then, everyone in town had heard about the fire, and locals came by to express their sympathy for the loss of the building. When the very first person handed Arnie a five-dollar bill, he looked at him curiously.

"To help you rebuild," the man said.

Arnie knew this person didn't have much money. "That's very kind of you, but I can't take this from you," Arnie said, trying to hand it back.

The man shook his head. "It's what neighbors do."

Edna experienced the same thing with many of the visitors. People handed her fives, tens, and even fifty-dollar bills. She tried explaining that they had insurance that would hopefully cover rebuilding the lodge, but everyone was adamant. "You'll need it," they all said. She was stunned at everyone's generosity.

"This would never have happened in L.A.," Arnie told Edna. "The people here are so generous."

She had to agree.

"Now what?" Edna asked Arnie that evening.

"We rebuild," he said.

"Do you think our insurance will cover it?" she asked. "We didn't update the insurance when we added on the additions."

"Then we'll start with one building again and keep going," Arnie said with determination. "It's all we can do."

A week later, after speaking with the insurance agent and getting a quote on what they would pay, Arnie searched for a contractor to build the new lodge. Arnie was a carpenter by trade and could even draw up designs if necessary, but he thought he should do this the right way this time. The first building had been very old, and the electrical had been wired incorrectly. The fire marshal had determined that the fire began with faulty wiring in the kitchen. This time, the lodge would be wired properly.

But when Arnie got a couple of estimates for rebuilding, he was stunned at the price.

"I could buy wood for a building twice the size and build it myself for the cost of a contractor," Arnie complained to Edna one evening. "It's highway robbery what they're charging."

"Then why don't you?" Edna asked him. They were sitting in front of the fireplace in their cottage, and the kids were already tucked away in bed.

Arnie stared at her in disbelief. "Because I'm not a professional contractor," he sputtered. "I just know how to build things."

Edna laughed. "Yes, you know how to build things. Big things, like houses and lodges. Put aside enough money for an electrician and plumber, and you build the rest. Like you said, we could have a much bigger lodge that way."

Arnie liked the idea, but one thing bothered him. "If I do it myself, it will take months, if not a year or so to build it. I could never afford to hire people to help. We'd be without an income for a long time. But if I hire a contractor, it could be done by fall at the latest, and we'd be open for hunting and the holidays."

Edna stared into the fire a moment, considering this. "Okay. If we pay a contractor, we'll have it sooner, but we'll have fewer rooms for guests. If you build it, it'll take longer, but we'll earn more money once it's finished. I vote for you building it."

Arnie sat back against the sofa. "You got me there." He smiled at Edna. "Okay, then. I guess we're going to build it ourselves."

Arnie got to work drawing up a new design for the lodge.

The stone fireplace had survived the fire—it just needed a good washing to remove the soot. So Arnie decided to create the living area where it had been with the kitchen behind it. There would still be rooms upstairs, but he made the building longer in the back to accommodate twelve rooms instead of six. They'd also have a dining room on the left of the staircase, and there would be access to that from the kitchen, too. His mind was a whirl of ideas as he planned how to create a rustic yet inviting-looking lodge for their guests.

In all, Arnie designed a place with twelve rooms in the lodge and sixteen rooms in the additions attached to the back. There'd be two large windows in the main living area and one in the dining room to let in plenty of sunshine all year round. When he showed his design to Edna, her eyes filled with tears.

"It's so beautiful," she said, wiping tears that fell down her cheeks. "It'll be so much nicer than the old building."

He agreed. But he also knew it would take a long time to build it.

Arnie ordered the wood and other supplies to be delivered and cleaned up the wreckage of the old lodge while he waited for it. The foundation was intact, as were the foundations for the additions he'd added before the fire. He had to lay cement between the additions and the new lodge to connect them, and then he was on his way to begin building.

May arrived, and the weather was a little warmer, making it easier to work outdoors. The first day Arnie planned to start working, he was surprised to find four men waiting for him at the worksite.

"Hey, guys. Why are you here?" he asked, noting they wore work boots and toolbelts and looked ready to build.

"We heard you were starting today," one of the men said.

Arnie knew his name was Grant, and he worked at the ski resort during the winter. "So, we're here to help you frame the new lodge."

Arnie could hardly believe his ears. "That's very nice of you guys, but I'm afraid I can't afford to pay for help."

"We aren't looking to be paid," Grant said. "We're here to help a neighbor."

Edna had come out to see what was happening and heard what Grant said. A lump formed in her throat. It was such a generous thing to do.

"Don't you men have to be at work?" Edna asked. She'd hate for them to lose a day's pay just to help them.

"No, ma'am," Grant said. "We all work at the ski resort, but that's closed until November. We work for the forestry all summer, but that doesn't start for another two weeks. So, we definitely have time to help."

Edna turned to Arnie as he looked at her. She knew he was thinking the same thing as she was. They certainly couldn't refuse their generous offer.

"Thank you, guys," Arnie said. "Your help will make all the difference."

Grant smiled. He was a large man with a crewcut and round face. "Happy to help. So, what do you want us to do?"

Grant and the other men came all that week, and then a few other men appeared on days they could help, too. Edna made lunch for the men and made sure they had clean water to drink all day long. Before they knew it, the new lodge was framed and ready for the interior to be framed.

Much to their surprise, Albert Henley—one of their favorite holiday guests and friends—and his nine-year-old son, George, showed up to help with the lodge for an entire week.

"I can't believe you're here," Edna said, hugging Albert and George.

"Well, we had to make sure our favorite holiday vacation spot would be open in time for Christmas," Albert said cheerfully. "And George wanted to help."

She insisted they stay at the cottage so he wouldn't have to pay for a hotel, and Albert and George jumped right in to help. Every day, at least three or four men showed up to help, and after a month of hard work, the lodge was built and ready for the plank siding and shingles on the roof. By July, Edna was painting the interior walls that didn't have wood planking on them and decorating each bedroom and bathroom. The local furniture shop gave them deep discounts on beds and other furniture since they had to order in bulk, which helped them immensely. By the end of August, the lodge was ready for fall visitors.

But first, Edna and Arnie invited everyone who volunteered their time to a big barbeque dinner for them and their families. They wanted to show their appreciation for everything everyone had done.

"We couldn't have done this without all of you," Arnie said, lifting his beer up in a toast. "Thank you all for your generosity and kind spirits. You truly are wonderful neighbors, and I hope someday I can help you too."

Everyone, even the kids, raised their glasses. Arnie's words moved Edna to tears, as it had many of the other people who'd attended.

That evening, after everyone had left and the kids were in bed, Arnie and Edna walked up to the lodge and stood staring at it under the moonlight.

"It really is a beautiful place," Edna said. "You built a lovely new lodge."

"We built a lovely new lodge," Arnie said. "The entire community did."

They stood in the moonlight for a long time, admiring their new building. Then they walked home, holding hands, looking forward to a busy workday the next day and every day after that.

Chapter Six

Today - Christmas Eve

Cassie was running from the moment she woke up. She was putting out little fires everywhere. She sent one of the kitchen staff into town when they ran short on supplies and had to call the liquor store again to ask where their champagne order was. Jen cleaned rooms again so Cassie could manage the front desk. There were so many guests who wanted rides up to the ski resort, and Gabe was the only driver. There was another shuttle bus in the lodge's garage, but there was no one to drive it.

"When can we get a ride to the ski resort?" yet another guest asked Cassie. "We want to be back in time for the Christmas dinner."

"Our driver is doing the best he can," she told the man. "I'm so sorry. We're short-staffed."

Cassie could tell the man was upset, but he didn't say so. She knew she'd be upset if the place where she was staying didn't have enough people to support the guests' needs.

Jen came back to the front desk. "Anything I can do?"

"Yes," Cassie said. "Please watch the desk while I drive a

few guests to the ski resort."

"You? Drive the shuttle bus?" Jen looked at Cassie in dismay.

"What? I used to drive it when I was eighteen."

"Yeah, but those are Gabe's babies. He'll be angry when he sees you driving it," Jen said.

Cassie frowned. "That may be so, but I own them; he doesn't. Please call the Johnson's room and tell them the bus will be ready to take them in ten minutes." Cassie grabbed the keys for the bus from the hook under the desk and headed to the lodge's back door. She took her coat from the rack at the back door and walked across the courtyard to the garage. The shuttle bus started up easily, and she carefully drove it around to the front of the lodge and waited for the Johnsons.

Gabe drove up at that moment, and his eyes grew wide. He hurled himself out of the other shuttle bus and strode up to Cassie. "Just what do you think you're doing?"

"I'm driving guests to the ski resort," she said.

"No, you're not. I'm back. I can take them," Gabe said.

Cassie's eyes narrowed. Who was he to tell her what she could and couldn't do? "You're needed at the airport in fifteen minutes to pick up guests."

"Then you go to the airport, and I'll go to the ski resort. Those roads are slippery."

The Johnsons were coming out the door with their ski equipment. They saw the two buses and looked at Cassie for guidance.

"Come in here," she said, opening the doors. "Be careful with your skis."

"Get out of the driver's seat," Gabe said. "I'll take them."

"No. Stop arguing with me," Cassie shouted. The family boarding the bus stared at her. "It's okay," she told them calmly.

"Come on in, and we'll take off." To Gabe, she said quietly, "We have a packed house with a big dinner and celebration tonight. People will want to go to town for last-minute items, go skiing, or need to be picked up at the airport. You can't do it all. Just let me help, okay?"

Gabe's face looked like he was going to explode. But after a moment, he relaxed and finally said, "Fine. You win." He went back to the other bus and drove off.

Cassie rolled her eyes and looked up in the rearview mirror. "Everyone ready? Let's go."

She drove several people around town and picked up families from the ski resort. It was a busy day, and Gabe had been right—the roads to the ski resorts were icy. But she was fine. It was like she was eighteen again, driving guests around. She actually loved it.

Later, back at the lodge, Cassie checked on the last-minute preparations and made sure the tables in the dining room looked festive. Then she went back to her house to change for dinner.

Cassie quickly showered and pulled her hair up in a messy bun. Then she carefully applied make-up. Generally, she wore very little make-up, but this was a special occasion.

Going through her closet, she picked a red dress she'd brought along for the Christmas celebration. It wasn't too tight but hugged her curves perfectly. It was sleeveless, so she put on the short, red bolero jacket that went with it. After slipping on a pair of black pumps, she gazed at herself in the mirror.

"Not too shabby," she told her reflection. Then she laughed at herself. Cassie dressed up often for events and dinners with clients. But tonight, it was fun to dress up for the annual Christmas celebration.

Just as she slipped her phone into her tiny purse, it beeped. Cassie had left her earbuds out of her ears for tonight. With a sigh, she answered the phone.

"Hi, Colleen. Merry Christmas. What can I do for you?" She listened as the actress had a full-out breakdown over something TMZ had said about her on television. Cassie didn't understand why a show like that existed just to put down celebrities, and she couldn't understand why Colleen watched it.

"Listen, Colleen. I'm sorry they said that. You shouldn't pay attention to them—or ever watch them. This is what they do. They put stuff out there that hurts other people. You know the truth about yourself, and that's all that matters."

Tearfully, Colleen begged her to come over.

"I'm sorry, Colleen, but I can't come over. I'm in Big Bear, at my family's resort. Aren't you with family?"

Cassie shook her head as she listened to Colleen. The poor woman had everything, yet nothing at all. "Okay. What about your boyfriend? Are you going to spend Christmas with him?"

Cassie's mind was spinning. Who could she call to go and calm Colleen down? The poor woman was spiraling out of control. It was Christmas Eve. She didn't want to call her assistant, Marcie, to drive over there. That wouldn't be fair. And apparently, Colleen's boyfriend was out of the picture.

"Colleen, dear. You need to calm down. I'm sorry I can't run over there tonight, and honestly, there's no one who can. It's the holidays, honey. But I won't hang up until I know you're okay." So, Cassie sat on the phone with Colleen for over an hour, knowing she would miss half of dinner. But it couldn't be helped. Even Colleen's therapist wouldn't answer the phone on Christmas Eve.

Finally, Colleen calmed down. She said she'd go to her

parents' house the next day and she'd be okay until then. After hanging up, Cassie rushed out of the house to go to the lodge and was surprised to see Gabe sitting there in his truck.

"Need a lift?" he asked with a smirk.

Cassie pulled herself up into the cab and smiled at him. He looked handsome in a dark suit with a white shirt and red satin tie. "I'm glad you're here, but why are you?" she asked.

"When you didn't show up for dinner, I came to get you. I figured you were on the phone with one of your crazies," Gabe said.

"Well, you were right, but my clients aren't crazy. Collen was having an emotional breakdown. I couldn't leave her hanging," Cassie said.

"And that's the difference between you and me. You're sweet, and I'm not." Gabe grinned again and took off toward the lodge.

There was still plenty of food at the buffet when Cassie and Gabe arrived, and they filled their plates. Cassie smiled and waved at guests who'd been coming to the lodge for years or who came as children and now had children of their own. As she sat at the head table with Gabe and Jen with her husband and kids, Cassie felt happy. She'd forgotten how much she'd enjoyed these holiday celebrations at the lodge. Jen's children were already enjoying dessert as Cassie and Gabe began eating. There was a separate table set up with cookies, cakes, and other sweet treats for everyone to enjoy.

"That cake looks delicious," Cassie said to two-year-old Emmie. "Is it as good as it looks?"

Emmie nodded excitedly while taking a huge bite. Chocolate cake smeared all over her little face.

"Ugh! It had to be chocolate," Jen said, trying to wipe

dessert off her little girl's face.

"That's the fun of Christmas," Gabe said.

Cassie moved closer to Gabe and spoke quietly. "Do they celebrate at the place where your father lives?"

Gabe nodded. "They're having a Christmas Eve dinner and gifts under the tree in the commons area. I'll stop by and see him tomorrow for a while between shuttling guests."

"I can help you drive guests around again, so you'll have time," Cassie offered.

Gabe pretended to glare at her, then laughed. "Sorry about the tantrum today. It seems like we keep getting into childish fights."

"We?" Cassie asked. "Seems to me you always start them."

"No, I don't," he said.

"Yes, you do," she countered. They stared at each other for a moment and started laughing.

"Just like the good old days," Gabe said.

After dinner, the guests gathered in the living area where more chairs had been added to accommodate everyone. Champagne was poured into flutes for those who wanted it, and hot apple cider was offered also. Someone started playing the piano by the fireplace, and soon, everyone joined in singing Christmas carols.

"Your mother would be so proud of you," an elderly lady said as she passed Cassie. "Keeping this tradition is what brings the guests back year after year."

"Thank you," Cassie said, suddenly feeling a pang at the loss of her mother. It was odd not having her here celebrating with all of them.

"Another perfect holiday celebration," George said to Cassie as he stood beside her. "Now, if we could just turn out the lights and light candles instead, it would be magical." He winked at her, then wandered off to where his family was.

"It's hard, isn't it?" Gabe said, coming up beside her and handing her another flute of champagne.

She knew what he meant. "Yes. My mother wasn't a fan of this lodge, but this was her favorite time of year here."

"I miss her too," Gabe said.

Cassie placed her hand on his arm and squeezed. "I know."

After a time, gifts from under the tree were handed out to each child. The gifts weren't expensive, but the children enjoyed them just the same. Since trees were in every guest room, families could celebrate their own Christmas in the morning with each other.

Soon, the guests began to disperse to their rooms, everyone wishing a Merry Christmas to each other. It had been another lovely holiday celebration at the lodge. Cassie tried to help clean up, but the employees shooed her away. She'd done enough already, they told her. She didn't argue. It had been another long day, and she was tired.

After saying goodbye to Jen and her family at the front door, Cassie walked outside for a moment. It was cold, and the snow had started to fall. But she loved looking at the lodge with its lit-up windows and holiday decorations.

Gabe joined her and placed her coat over her shoulders. "It's cold out here, silly. We can't afford for you to get sick."

She chuckled. "Thank you. You know, I forgot how much I loved this place in the winter. It's hard to believe that, only two hours away, it's warm with no snow. L.A. isn't magical at Christmas."

"No, it isn't. But you don't have to plow the driveway or shovel the sidewalks, either," Gabe teased.

"True. But honestly, there's nothing magical about L.A., ever."

"What about Hollywood and all those glittering movie stars? Are you saying they're not magical?" Gabe asked, pretending to look shocked.

"Oh, stop it." Cassie shoved him playfully as he laughed. Growing serious, she looked him in the eye. "Did anyone tell you that you look quite handsome tonight?"

He stood there rubbing his beard as if thinking. "Let me see. I think that elderly lady said I looked rather fine."

Cassie rolled her eyes.

"Thank you," he said, no longer teasing. "But it's you who looked beautiful tonight. But then, you look beautiful even when you're plunging a toilet."

"Okay, that's enough of you," Cassie said. "Please take me home." She started walking toward the front door to go inside when Gabe grabbed her arm and turned her around to face him.

Cassie looked up into his eyes and saw something she hadn't seen in a long time—desire. Gabe's eyes made her knees nearly melt as he held her there, his face inches from hers. When he lowered his lips to hers, she didn't protest. His kiss was everything she'd remembered it to be—even better—since they were teenagers the last time their lips touched. She could have kissed him all night.

Gabe was the first to pull away, and he gave her a small smile. "Mistletoe," he said, glancing up.

"What?" Cassie looked up, and there, hanging from the entryway's rafters, was mistletoe. "Hm. I wonder who hung that there," she said, then smiled.

"Some plaid-covered elf, I suppose," he said, finally letting her go and stepping back. "I'll take you home."

Cassie nodded. But she was sorry the moment between them was over and felt guilty for feeling that way.

Chapter Seven

Today - Christmas Day

Cassie awoke the next day feeling off-balanced. It wasn't because of the champagne the night before, though. It was because of Gabe's kiss.

As she hurried from her house to the lodge, Cassie was trying to figure out if she was angry with Gabe or okay with what he'd done. Gabe knew she was engaged, but he'd kissed her anyway. Although, Cassie hadn't discouraged him either. In fact, she'd enjoyed the kiss and had even wanted it.

Ugh! She was just as guilty as Gabe.

Jared was at the desk when she arrived because Cassie had insisted that Jen have all of Christmas Day off. After checking what needed to be done first, Cassie decided to go on room cleaning duty before checking to see if they needed a second driver today.

Grabbing a tray of cleaning supplies from the closet and putting an apron on over her clothes, Cassie exited the little room in such a hurry that she ran smack dab into someone's hard chest.

"Oh, I'm so sorry," she said, looking up. Gabe smiled down at her.

"I'm not. You can run into me anytime," he said.

Cassie wanted to be angry but couldn't. He stood there grinning, which only made her smile too. "Let me know when you want to visit your dad, and I'll take over shuttle bus duty," she told him.

"I'm going at noon for a little bit," he said. "I told Jared not to book any shuttle bus activity between noon and one. I knew you'd be busy with other things."

"Oh. Okay. That was smart," she said.

"Would you like to come along and see him?" Gabe offered. "I can't promise he'll remember you, or it will be more fun than cleaning toilets, but I'm sure he'd love to see you."

Cassie thought for a moment. She would like to see Mitch, but she also had a lot of work to do. *Give yourself a break,* the voice inside her head told her. "Yes. I'd love to see your dad. I'll meet you out front at noon."

Gabe nodded and headed off in the opposite direction from Cassie. She'd hoped to talk to him about last night and what it all meant—if anything. But maybe it was best to let it go.

As she walked to the first room that needed cleaning, Cassie called Colleen to check on her. She'd felt bad that Colleen had such a terrible night last night, and she couldn't be there for her.

"Hello? Colleen? How are you feeling today?" Cassie asked when the young starlet answered. Colleen's voice sounded calmer, and she actually sounded happy.

"I'm so happy you and your boyfriend are back together," Cassie said. She knew that if someone was around for Colleen, the woman would call her less. "You have a great holiday."

Feeling better, Cassie pulled a cart full of room supplies out of a maid's closet and made her way to the first room that needed cleaning.

At noon, Cassie was waiting at the door for Gabe to drive up. He did seconds later in his old pick-up truck, and she climbed inside.

"Did you get everything spotless clean?" Gabe asked, glancing at her mischievously.

"You really like making fun of me cleaning rooms, don't you? You know, it's a respectable way to earn a living," Cassie said.

"I absolutely agree," he said. "Remember, I fix stuffed-up toilets." He chuckled. "It's just that you don't seem the type to clean up after others. I bet you have a maid come in to clean up your messes at home."

"I don't pay a maid," she said, then added, "Blake does. We live in his apartment."

"Oh." Gabe kept his eyes on the road. "I wanted to talk to you about last night. I'm sorry I kissed you. I shouldn't have done that because I know you're engaged. I hope you don't hold it against me."

She stared at him a moment, wondering if his apology was sincere or if he was just being polite. "Are you really sorry?" she asked.

He looked at her sideways. "A little. I mean, it was a heck of a kiss."

"That's what I thought," she told him. "But thanks for trying to apologize."

"Anytime."

They pulled up in front of a one-story building that had large windows and was painted dark green with brown trim.

With the pines and shrubs around it, the place looked very homey. Cassie followed Gabe inside, where he waved to a nurse and then entered the commons area. A large tree stood in the corner near a gas fireplace, and comfortable sofas and chairs were placed strategically around the room, creating small sitting areas. Gabe went directly to the front corner of the room, where an elderly man with thick, silver-gray hair sat in a wheelchair. From his spot, he could see both the tree and the crackling fireplace.

"Hi, Dad. It's Gabe," he said softly as he stepped in front of his father. "Merry Christmas."

Cassie stood beside Gabe, watching the elderly gentleman. It had been a few years since she'd seen Mitch, and she was shocked to see how old he'd become. She remembered when he first had tremors in his hands years ago, but he'd always brushed it off as being nothing but old age. Now, his whole body shook, and his eyes looked vacant.

"Hi, Mitch. Remember me?" she asked cheerfully. "It's Cassie. I'm so happy to see you."

Mitch's eyes had moved just a bit as if he were looking at Cassie, but there was no recognition in them.

Gabe moved his father's wheelchair to face one of the sofas, and he and Cassie sat down. "I see you got the new sweater I brought you for Christmas," Gabe said. "I remembered that you liked dark blue." Gabe waited a moment, then said, "I hope the robe fit too. You really needed a new one."

Mitch didn't move or respond. He just sat there, still staring at the fire.

Gabe turned to Cassie. "Sorry. It's rare for him to say anything these days. They've tried different medications, but nothing works."

Cassie saw the sadness in Gabe's eyes. She reached for his hand and squeezed it. "That's okay. I'm just happy to see Mitch again."

After a while, they wished Mitch a Merry Christmas and left, still holding hands. Cassie wasn't even conscious of them touching until they had to break apart when they reached the truck.

"I'm sorry about your dad," she said to Gabe when they got inside the truck. "But I'm glad you made sure he was in a nice place. He's being well taken care of."

Gabe nodded, his jaw tightening. Cassie knew that look. If he wasn't clenching his teeth, he'd probably break down and cry, and crying wasn't something Gabe wanted to do in front of her or anyone.

After they parted at the lodge, they were both so busy they didn't see each other until dinner that night. A festive Christmas dinner was served in the dining room for the guests, and there were delicious desserts to choose from. Knowing they'd have three different celebrations through New Year's, Cassie had brought a different dress for each night. Tonight, she wore a black dress with silver threads running through the fabric. It had a tight bodice and full skirt, and the silver shimmered under the lights. She paired her black heels with it and left her hair down with soft curls created with her curling iron. When she arrived at their table, she saw Gabe's eyes light up. He instantly stood and pulled out her chair for her.

"Thank you," she said, surprised by his old-fashioned manners.

"You look lovely tonight," he whispered in her ear before sitting down again.

A shiver ran down her spine. She wasn't sure if it was from

his compliment or if the room was cold. Considering she had a fiancé, she blamed it on the cold.

After dinner, the guests stood and chatted in the living area while having a nightcap. Cassie mingled around the room, talking to guests she'd known her entire life and new guests who'd just started coming to the lodge.

"It's such a shame this place is closing," an elderly woman said to Cassie. "Our family loves coming here each Christmas. Have you had anyone interested in buying it yet?"

"Not yet," Cassie said. "But we're hoping someone will buy it soon. I'd love to see it open by the holidays next year."

"My, my, but don't you look pretty tonight." George walked up to Cassie. "And what a wonderful job you've done of the holidays this year. Becky and I plan on staying through New Year's Eve for the celebration. We wouldn't miss it for the world."

"I'm so happy you'll be here," Cassie said.

Gabe came over to stand beside Cassie. "Tell us another of your stories about the lodge," Gabe said. "I never tire of them."

George became all smiles. "Well, there was that time, in the spring of 1970, I believe, that the lodge caught on fire in the middle of the night."

The other guests began to circle them, wanting to hear the story.

"I wasn't here," George said. "But Arnie and Edna told us what had happened. Your grandmother smelled smoke and got out of bed to check the fireplace in the cottage where they lived, right behind the lodge. That's when she saw the lodge was on fire."

Cassie shivered. She'd heard this story from both her grandmother and her mother before, but the thought of the lodge burning down was still scary for her.

"She woke Arnie up, and he called the head of the volunteer fire department. But it was too late," George said. "By the time they arrived, the lodge was nearly burned down." He shook his head. "Poor Arnie. He'd recently built new additions to the lodge, and it was all gone. Luckily, their cottage didn't catch on fire, so they had a place to live."

The guests listening to the story all shook their heads and murmured how tragic losing the lodge must have been.

"Luckily, my grandfather did have insurance on the lodge," Cassie added. "But he was afraid it would take him a year to rebuild it, and they'd lose a lot of income."

"That's right," George said. "When Arnie found out hiring a contractor would cost him twice as much as building the lodge himself, he decided that's what he'd do. And to his surprise, the day he began framing the exterior, several men showed up to help. Throughout the summer, men came every day that they didn't have to go to work and helped him. Arnie was so surprised that his neighbors would do that for him, he said he could have cried."

"He was touched by everyone's generosity," Cassie said, remembering her grandfather telling her about rebuilding. "He'd never experienced people giving of themselves for a neighbor before."

George nodded. "And when Edna called us to cancel our holiday reservation, my father took a week off of work to come and help, too. I begged my dad to come with him, and he actually let me take off of school to come. I was so proud to be able to help rebuild the lodge with all the grown men."

Cassie smiled. "We have a photo of everyone," she said, leaving the room for a moment. She returned with a large, framed photo that hung on the entryway wall. Everyone crowded around her to get a good look. "This is you here, isn't it, George?"

"Why yes, it is," George said proudly. "And much to Arnie and Edna's surprise, the lodge was built and completed in time for the fall season and winter holidays. It was a happy ending to what could have been a sad story."

"That's a great memory, George," Gabe said. "Stories like that make the lodge special. I'll miss that when it closes down."

George nodded. "I sure will miss this place." He glanced over at Cassie. "But I understand, too. Nothing lasts forever."

Cassie gave the older man a sweet kiss on the cheek as she walked back to the entryway to hang up the picture. She gazed at it a moment, then at the others that hung there. The photos depicted the many years the lodge had been standing. Her grandfather and grandmother, then her father and mother after them, had made this place the success it was. It was her legacy. And she hadn't realized how hard it would be for her to let it go.

"Hey. Are you okay?" a male voice said from behind her. She didn't have to turn to see who it was. She knew Gabe's voice well.

"I'm fine. I was just looking at all the photos of the lodge through the years," Cassie said.

Gabe moved closer beside her. "You know, these hang here year after year, yet I never really look at them. I know they're here, but I don't give them the appreciation they deserve."

"I know what you mean. I never really took the lodge seriously, either, until now. It's easy for me to ignore its existence when I'm living in L.A. But now, I'm watching my family's business go away. It's hard."

"You can always decide to keep it open," Gabe said gently. "A good manager, like Jen, and of course, me, would run it like it belonged to us."

"I don't know, Gabe." She looked at him. "I know the place would be in good hands with you two, but it still would be my responsibility. My mind would be here when I was in L.A. and in L.A. when I was here. I can't do that to myself."

"Do you love living in L.A. that much?" Gabe asked. "I mean, you could make a good living with the lodge."

"I've worked really hard to get where I am in the firm," she said. "I'm one of the youngest PR agents with some of the biggest clients. How can I give that up?"

Gabe nodded. "I get it. I do. I'm sure you've worked hard." He smiled. "But I can always hope you'll come home."

"Home," Cassie said longingly. "I couldn't get out of here fast enough when I was eighteen. But now, it's still home to me."

Gabe reached over and tucked a stray strand of her blond hair behind her ear. The gesture was so simple, yet so intimate, that Cassie's heart pounded.

"I'd better go help clean the place up for the night," Cassie said, backing away. The last thing she needed was to melt into Gabe's arms again.

"Let everyone else clean it up," Gabe said huskily. "It's late, and you've had a long day. I'll drive you back to your house."

Cassie let out a long sigh. She was tired. So very tired. "Okay. Thanks."

"No thanks necessary," he said, smiling. He went to get her coat, and they walked out into the night to his truck.

Chapter Eight

Christmas 1975

Edna was worried. She'd been worrying a lot lately. It was only a week until Christmas, and the lodge still had several available rooms. The entire year had been slow, thanks to the recession, but she'd hoped their regular guests would fill the lodge up through the holidays. Unfortunately, she was wrong.

Sighing, Edna stood at the front desk and reviewed their accounting books once more. The past two years, Arnie had continued to add on to the lodge and had even put in his much-wanted pool in the back courtyard. It had been expensive. And last year, he took a mortgage out on the lodge to build their private house at the back of the property. Edna had told him she didn't need a big, expensive home, but he'd built one anyway.

"I'm saving us a lot of money by building it myself," Arnie had said. But the truth was, he'd hired several other men to help so it would be finished by winter. Edna hated having that mortgage against the lodge because if business didn't pick up, they could lose everything.

"Why the long face?" Arnie asked his wife after dropping an armload of wood into the box by the fireplace. "It's nearly Christmas. You should be happy."

Edna frowned at him. "We aren't booked up this year. I don't think it'll be a very profitable holiday season."

Arnie waved his hand through the air as if to brush off her concern. "Life isn't always about money," he said gently. "We'll be okay."

Anger rose inside of her. Arnie just didn't understand. Last summer, they'd hired a high school kid, Mitch Kessler, part-time to help Arnie with all the extra maintenance work around the place and to drive guests to and from the ski resorts and town. Plus, they'd had to hire two women to clean rooms each day because Edna could no longer keep up. The cost of paying employees was eating into their small profits. Arnie didn't seem to understand that the bigger he built the lodge, the more help they needed—and that cost money.

The phone rang before she could say another word to her husband. Edna hoped it was someone wanting to make a last-minute booking for the holidays.

Later that evening, as they sat in their home far behind the lodge, Edna made Arnie go over the books with her so he could see why she was worried. Their son, Craig, now fifteen, was managing the front desk until ten, and their daughter, Amanda, now thirteen, was in her room doing homework. At least, that's what Edna believed she was doing. Knowing her youngest, she was probably on the phone with her best friend, talking about boys.

"See this here?" Edna said, pointing to the cost of the mortgage on the house and the lodge's expenses. "This is more than we're taking in. Our savings are dwindling to nothing. I can't take money from it anymore to make up the difference. If we don't fill up for the holidays, our January payment for the house will be late."

Arnie stared at the numbers in disbelief. "But we have more rooms than two years ago and more to offer guests. I don't get it. Why aren't we making enough money?"

"Because we also have three employees that we didn't have two years ago, as well as a mortgage payment. Now, we have to fill the place up all winter just to pay the bills," Edna said.

Arnie shrugged. "I'm sure if we miss one payment the bank will understand. It's not the end of the world, sweetheart. We can make up for it later on."

"With what?" Edna asked. "You know as well as I do that after New Year's Eve, it slows down around here. Sure, we get skiers, but it's not as packed as November and December. And summer is busy, but even the summers have had fewer guests these past two years. No one has any money. The economy is causing people to tighten up on their spending. We should have been more careful."

Arnie stared at her, stunned. "But I thought you wanted a new house."

"I did. But I told you we couldn't afford it. We could have lived in the cottage a couple of more years."

"I promised you a house when we bought the lodge, and I wanted to keep my promise," Arnie said. "I'm sure things will get better. We'll just have to be a little careful."

Edna sighed. "I'm going crazy trying to be careful, Arnie. I've been juggling the income and expenses for two years now. We have to do more than be careful—we have to cut back a lot."

"Where?" Arnie asked.

"I think we should cancel the Christmas celebration dinner this year and the New Year's Eve celebration, too," Edna said. "The food, champagne, and the gifts for the kids are so expensive. We can suggest other places for the guests to eat on Christmas Eve instead."

Arnie's mouth dropped open. "We can't do that. Our regulars expect us to have celebrations. We've always done it."

"But we can't afford it," Edna said, growing more frustrated. "The only other alternative is to charge more for the rooms or charge for the meal."

"No!" Arnie stood and walked over to the fireplace. "No. This has always been our gift to our loyal customers, and I won't stop doing it now. We'll do the best we can. But we're not going to cancel."

Edna's heart pounded with anger. How could he not see they were on the brink of losing everything? She stood and slammed the accounts book shut. "Fine. Do it your way. But don't say I didn't warn you when the bank comes and takes everything away." Edna stormed off into their bedroom, slamming the door.

The next few days were strained between Arnie and Edna. They'd had fights in the seventeen years they'd been married, but they'd always been able to fix things in an hour or two. Never had they not talked to each other for days.

Every time the phone rang, Edna prayed it was for a room booking. They had a few last-minute Christmas bookings because the other resorts and hotels in town were already full. But they still had several rooms open, and Edna feared they'd never fill them.

On the third day after their fight, a dejected-looking Arnie approached the desk and asked, "Would you like me to go into town and pick up the gifts for the guests' children? Then you won't have to make time for it."

Edna knew he was trying to make up for their fight, but she also knew he'd have no idea what to buy young children. "No, that's fine. I'll do it this afternoon."

"Is there anything I can do to help?" he asked.

"Everything is planned," Edna snapped, then returned to working on the receipts. From the corner of her eye, Edna saw her husband walk away sadly. She knew she should get over their argument and make up, but she wasn't ready to. She just couldn't. All she did was worry about money, and Arnie wasn't being serious about it. It made her angry all over again just thinking about it.

While Edna was away buying the gifts, she put Craig in charge of the desk. She quickly picked up small items for each child on her list and bought extra wrapping paper, too. It wasn't a lot of money, but it was still more than they should have been spending.

When she returned to the lodge, Craig called her over.

"Mom. You have to call this man back. He wanted to book a bunch of rooms, and I didn't want to mess it up," Craig said.

"Really?" Edna became excited. "Why don't you see if you can help your father outside," she told Craig, and he hurried off to put on his coat and boots to go outside. Edna set her bags behind the desk and carefully dialed the number Craig had written down. "Hello?" she said. "Is this Mr. Johanneson? I'm calling from the Mountain View Lodge in Big Bear."

Edna listened as the man told her he was looking for several rooms for the week of Christmas through the New Year. The man booked all the available rooms before hanging up. Edna squealed with excitement.

Arnie came running in from the kitchen. "What happened? What's the matter?" He looked so scared that it made Edna laugh.

"I just booked the remainder of the rooms for Christmas week. I can't believe it. We're going to be full!" Edna said excitedly.

Arnie's face changed from fear to excitement. "That's wonderful. He ran around the desk and pulled Edna into his arms, lifting her up and twirling her around. She laughed at his silliness.

After he'd set her down, Arnie looked at her seriously. "Are we okay?" he asked softly.

Edna nodded. "Yes. We're okay. This doesn't solve all our problems, but it will greatly help."

Arnie smiled wide. When he smiled like this, Edna thought he looked as boyishly handsome as when she'd first met him. He kissed her sweetly and then headed toward the kitchen. "We'll need a bigger turkey," he called out as he left the room.

Edna laughed. They'd definitely need a bigger turkey. Probably two turkeys.

That night in bed, Arnie reached for Edna's hand. "Let's never fight over money again," he said gently. "I'll do my best to be as frugal as possible and listen to you when you think we shouldn't spend money."

"Okay," Edna said. "I hate fighting about money too. We'll try to work better as a team."

Arnie rolled on his side and looked at her. "When we moved here, it was because I didn't want to live in the rat race anymore. Until our fight, I hadn't realized that I was creating my own stress here. I'm glad we have this nice house, but I won't put stress on our finances like this again."

"I'm glad to hear it," Edna said. "I love this house too. Let's just keep things as they are for the time being. I know you want the lodge to grow even bigger, but let's take baby steps. I don't want to be stressed either."

He kissed her to seal the deal. Edna was relieved they weren't fighting anymore.

That Christmas, many of their regulars came to celebrate as well as some new regular guests were made. The Johannesons were so happy with their stay that they immediately booked rooms for the following year. In the end, despite the cost, Edna was happy Arnie talked her into having the big Christmas dinner and celebration along with the gifts for all the guests' children. It wouldn't have seemed like Christmas if they'd canceled it.

"Thank you for keeping the tradition," Arnie whispered to her on Christmas Eve as everyone toasted the holiday with champagne. "It wouldn't be the same without it."

Edna smiled and clinked glasses with her husband, then kissed him. "I agree," she said softly. She knew they'd be okay as long as they were together. They'd survived the fire, and they would survive the recession. Being together was all that mattered.

Chapter Nine

Today – December 28th

The days between Christmas and New Year's Eve were speeding by for Cassie. She and Jen took turns between managing the desk and cleaning rooms. Cassie didn't mind doing the cleaning. She could let her mind wander while she vacuumed and mopped. It had been a long time since she'd done physical work, and it made the day go quicker than sitting at a desk taking endless calls from whiny celebrities.

Not that she still didn't get calls from her celebrity clients. Every day was a difficult day for Colleen, and RD and Joe were getting into trouble all the time. Frankly, cleaning up the guests' messes was easier than cleaning up her clients' mistakes.

Cassie also enjoyed driving the guests to the ski resort and around town. She saw people she hadn't seen in years and caught up with old friends from high school. It was fun being in a town where everyone knew each other instead of a place like L.A., which was so large she felt invisible.

"Getting those toilets nice and clean?" Gabe asked with a grin as he passed her in the hallway.

"Go change a lightbulb," she told him, which made him laugh. Teasing Gabe was half the fun of working at the lodge. Cassie had forgotten that she could actually have fun at work. She never had fun at her office. Everything there was always life or death.

Unfortunately, Cassie knew that after New Year's Eve, everything would end. The lodge would be closed, waiting for a buyer, and she'd return to her life and job in L.A. When she'd first arrived, she couldn't wait to go back. But now, she wasn't as eager to leave.

Three days before New Year's Eve, Cassie had just finished cleaning rooms and was back at the front desk to take over for Jen when a familiar face popped up. He smiled at her with perfectly straight teeth. "Surprise!"

"Blake?" Cassie was so stunned to see him that she just stared.

"I told you I'd come for New Year's Eve," he said cheerfully. His smile faded. "Wow. You look like you've been cleaning an attic or something."

Cassie looked down. Her clothes had dirt smudges on them, and her hair was falling out of its ponytail. "I have been cleaning," she said tightly.

"Well, no matter." Blake put on a big smile again. "I brought a surprise for you."

Cassie watched as a well-dressed man and beautiful woman entered the lodge, with Gabe coming up in the rear with all their suitcases. "What's going on?" Cassie asked Blake.

"Cassie. This is Trevor Kensington and his lovely wife, Renee. Trevor owns several resorts all over the U.S. When I told him the lodge was for sale, he was very interested."

"Hello," Trevor said, reaching out his hand to shake

Cassie's. "You must be Cassie. It's very nice to meet you."

Cassie shook his hand, still in shock. Interested in the lodge? Really? "It's nice to meet you, too," she said automatically.

"When Blake told me about this lovely lodge, I just had to come and see it. My wife and I have booked a room for two nights to get a chance to look it over."

Cassie glanced at Renee and suddenly felt like a scullery maid compared to her. Renee was tall and thin, like a fashion model, with long blond hair and eyes that looked unnaturally light blue. Renee stood there looking bored.

"Well, then," Cassie finally said. "Let me check you in."

"Me, too," Blake said. "I have a room also."

"Oh. I figured you'd stay at the house with me," Cassie said. Although she wouldn't have been opposed to him staying in a room instead.

"Oh. The house. Yes," Blake said. "I forgot about the family house on the premises."

Cassie checked in the Kensingtons and told Gabe the room number so he could show them the way. Gabe didn't look all that happy.

"Gabe?" Blake said, turning to look at him. "Cassie has talked about you. Haven't you been working here as the janitor since high school?"

Cassie saw Gabe tighten his jaw. He looked like he wanted to punch Blake. "Gabe is more like the caretaker of our beautiful lodge," she said. "He can fix anything here, and he keeps the place in such great shape."

"Oh," Blake said. He reached out his hand. "It's nice meeting you finally, Gabe."

Cassie stared at first Blake and then Gabe. Blake wore a cashmere sweater under his expensive down jacket and designer jeans. Gabe was in his usual Levi's, t-shirt, and plaid shirt. The two men couldn't have been more different.

"Sorry, my hands are full," Gabe said, still holding onto the Kensington's luggage. He turned to Trevor and Renee. "I'll take you to your room."

"Wonderful," Trevor said. "And Cassie, if you're available tonight for dinner, I'd like to talk about the lodge with you."

"Of course," Cassie said. She watched as Gabe led the way to the elevator that would take the Kensingtons to the upper-floor room that had the best view in the lodge.

Blake looked at his suitcase sitting on the floor near him. "Can someone take my luggage to the house?"

Cassie grabbed the keys to one of the shuttle buses. "I'll take you to the house so you can get settled in."

Blake's eyes nearly popped out of his head when Cassie got behind the wheel of the bus, but he kept silent. She drove the short distance to the house and led him inside.

"My room is upstairs if you want to put your suitcase in there," she said, walking to the fireplace and putting a few logs in it to restart the fire.

Blake followed her. "First things first," he said in his deep, sexy voice. He circled his arms around her, pulling her close, and kissed her deeply. Cassie didn't melt in his embrace. In fact, she didn't feel anything at all. After a moment, she pulled away.

Blake frowned. "Is something wrong?"

"Ah, no," she said hurriedly. "It's just that I know my clothes are dirty from working all day, and I'd hate to get dirt on your nice sweater."

"Oh." Blake glanced around while she closed the fireplace doors. "So this was your parents' house?"

"Yes," Cassie said.

"Hm. It's nice, I guess. If you like the '70s."

Cassie winced. "Sure, it was built in the 1970s, but my parents remodeled it through the years. I think it's nice."

"Of course it is," Blake said hurriedly. "Sorry, I didn't mean to insult you."

"Sorry," Cassie said, her anger abating. "I'm just tired. Why don't I show you to the room, and we can clean up for dinner. I have a feeling Trevor will want to go to a fancy restaurant tonight."

Cassie was right. Trevor suggested they go to Captains Anchorage for dinner because he'd heard good things about it from celebrities he knew. Gabe drove them there in the shuttle bus. As they all left the bus, Blake tried to give Gabe a tip, but Gabe waved it away.

"Sorry," Cassie said to Gabe, embarrassed that Blake had done that. "He really did mean well. He's so used to having to tip everyone in L.A."

"I get it," Gabe said. Then his frown turned into a smile. "You look beautiful tonight."

Cassie was so taken aback by the compliment that she felt a blush warm her face. "Thanks. It's the same dress I wore on Christmas. Nothing special."

"It looks special to me," Gabe said. "Call me when you're ready to be picked up."

"Okay." She walked down the three steps and then turned when Gabe said her name.

"Cassie? Don't sell the lodge for too little. Get as much as you can out of these people."

She stared into Gabe's eyes and saw how sad he looked. She understood how he felt. Cassie had thought selling the lodge would be easy, but now, after spending time here, she knew it wouldn't be easy at all.

"Coming?" Blake asked Cassie, reaching for her hand. She reluctantly accepted his hand and followed the group into the restaurant. She felt like she'd left a part of herself back on the bus.

The hostess smiled widely when she saw Cassie. "I'd heard you were in town, but I still can't believe it," the perky redhead said, coming around her small podium to hug Cassie. "I'm so happy to see you."

"Thanks, Rhonda. It's great seeing you, too," Cassie said, smiling at her old high school friend. "You look amazing."

"Thank you. You're just adorable—as always. I'll show you to your table." Rhonda picked up the menus and showed them to a round table in the corner of the room. "Watch out for George tonight," Rhonda said. "He's been full of mischief."

Blake stared at Cassie. "Who's George?"

Cassie laughed. "He's the resident ghost here. George causes all kinds of trouble."

Blake glanced around, a frown on his face, then looked at the menu.

"The rustic look is very popular around here, isn't it?" Trevor asked, gazing around.

"Well, many of these buildings have been here since the early 1900s," Cassie said. "Or have burnt down and been rebuilt in the same style. We're in the mountains, so of course, you're going to see a lot of log buildings."

"It must get tiring," Renee said, scrunching her nose.

"No, most tourists find it charming," Cassie said.

Trevor and Renee perused the menu, with Renee complaining that there were no vegetarian dishes. Cassie tried hard not to laugh—vegetarian? In the mountains? They were lucky there wasn't elk or venison on the menu.

After ordering, Trevor focused his attention on Cassie. "So. Tell me about the Mountain View Lodge. Blake said it's been in your family for years."

"Decades, actually," Cassie said. "My grandparents started it with an old log saloon that had rooms upstairs back in 1965."

"Really?" Trevor said. "The building doesn't look that old."

"No, it isn't," Cassie said. "Unfortunately, the original building burned down in 1970. But my grandfather and many of his friends rebuilt it, and then he added on through the years. The indoor pool was once an outdoor pool, but my father changed that and then added the outdoor infinity pool in the front years later. My parents also added more rooms and the spa at the back of the building."

"I like that you have a spa. It's perfect for bringing in celebrity clientele. Tomorrow, you'll have to give me a tour so I can see everything," Trevor said.

"Of course. I'd be happy to," Cassie told him.

Blake smiled at her and winked. She could tell he was very proud of himself for finding Trevor and bringing him here. Yet, Cassie wasn't as happy about it as she should be.

After dinner, Cassie called Gabe, and he came to pick them up. She thanked him profusely for driving them once they'd reached the lodge.

"Isn't that his job?" Blake asked right in front of Gabe.

"Gabe has been working since early this morning," Cassie told Blake sharply. "It was nice of him to stay on late and pick us up."

Blake's brows rose, but he didn't say another word. He followed Trevor instead as they looked around the lodge.

"You were a little harsh with your fiancé, don't you think?" Gabe asked.

Cassie sighed. "I don't know why, but he's getting on my nerves. There's just too much going on."

"I get it," Gabe said. "Just relax. It's only a couple more days, and we'll be closed."

"Or have a new owner," Cassie said.

"Maybe." Gabe headed out the entryway door to put the shuttle bus away.

"So, what's this I hear about a New Year's Eve celebration," Trevor asked Cassie when she caught up with them. They'd opened the dining room door, which was already set for breakfast.

"It's one of our yearly celebrations we have for our guests," Cassie said. "It's our way of thanking them for coming every year."

"Do you charge extra for it?" Trevor asked.

"No. That's the point. We do it for the guests," Cassie said.

"Hm. It seems like that would cut into profits."

"Well, it does, but not too much," Cassie told him. "You see, many of our guests have been coming here for years. Some are second-generation families that have come here for the holidays since 1966. We've always put on a Christmas Eve and a New Year's Eve celebration for them."

"Wow." Trevor gazed around the dining room. "It's wonderful to have return guests, but a place like this could easily charge for extra celebrations, and guests wouldn't mind. Not if they are that loyal."

Cassie stared at the slick-looking millionaire. *They won't be loyal to you,* she thought, but remained silent.

"Well, we're off to our room for the night," Trevor said,

placing his arm around his wife. "Shall we meet at ten tomorrow morning for the tour?"

"That'll be fine," Cassie said.

They said their goodnights, and then Cassie was left alone with Blake.

"I was thinking of getting a room here at the lodge for tonight after all," Blake said tentatively. "You seem so preoccupied; I think you'd sleep better if I was out of the way."

"You really don't have to do that," Cassie said, feeling bad for snapping at him earlier. Yet, she felt relieved that Blake wanted his own room.

He smiled and gently placed his hands on her arms. "I know what it's like to feel overwhelmed. And I know when you've had enough. Plus, I'll probably be on the phone half the night with the band guys. They have a New Year's Eve gig and are upset that I won't be there."

"Okay. Maybe you're right," Cassie said, feeling relieved. "I'm not sure if we have an open room, though."

Blake dropped his hands to his side. "I already checked with Jared at the front desk. He said there was a room I could use and that he'd be happy to run and get my luggage for me from the house."

"Okay. Great." Even though Cassie felt relieved, she felt a little dejected as well.

"I'm not angry," Blake said. "Please don't take it that way. You know I sleep better when I'm alone. Also," he hesitated, and his eyes went to her hand. "I noticed that you haven't been wearing your engagement ring. I hope that doesn't mean more than you just didn't want to lose it."

Cassie looked down at her hand and felt guilty. She'd forgotten all about putting her ring on. In fact, she hadn't missed it at all this week. "I was afraid I'd lose it when I was cleaning around here," she said.

Blake smiled. "I figured it was something like that." He kissed her chastely on the cheek. "Goodnight. I'll join you on the tour tomorrow, okay?"

"Yes. That's fine. Goodnight." Cassie watched as Blake went up the stairs and disappeared down the hallway. He must have gotten a room next to Trevor and his wife.

She went to the front desk and told Jared not to worry about Blake's luggage—she'd bring it over for him. Then she said goodnight and headed to the back door. Slipping on her coat, she walked outside and ran right into Gabe.

"Oh! You scared me!" she said. "Why aren't you home?"

Gabe chuckled. "Why aren't you home?"

This made Cassie laugh. "Because it was a long night. I'm heading there now."

Gabe frowned. "Where's the fiancé?"

"Stop calling him that, okay? He took a room. Apparently, I haven't been that nice."

"You? Not nice? I don't believe it," Gabe said, smirking. "Come on. I'll drive you home. It's cold out."

"Thanks. But I need to bring back Blake's suitcase," Cassie said.

"I'll bring it back and let Jared take it to him," Gabe said. "You need your beauty rest."

She gave him the evil eye as she got up into his truck. "Are you saying I look like an old hag?"

"Never. You look lovely," Gabe said softly.

Cassie looked up into his warm eyes and saw he wasn't teasing her. She didn't answer him. She was afraid of what she might say, and some things were better left unsaid.

Chapter Ten

Winter 1977

Amanda Burke stood outside on a blustery night, assisting skiers into the chair lifts that took them up the mountain. At fifteen years old, she was a tall, slender girl with long blond hair and bright blue eyes. But bundled up in ski bibs, a jacket, stocking cap, and a hood over her head, no one could tell just how cute she was.

"Hey. I'm supposed to take over for you. The owner said you can work at the snack bar for the rest of your shift," a teen boy called to her over the wind.

Amanda turned around and saw her classmate, Jonas Nichols. "Hi, Jonas. I knew you worked here, but I haven't seen you all season."

Jonas' eyes grew wide when he realized who he was talking to. "Amanda? What on earth are you doing working here? Don't you work for your parents at the lodge?"

Amanda laughed. Jonas looked funny with his wide-eyed Bambi look. "I do work for my parents, but they don't pay me. So I work here to earn a little money. I want my own car when

I turn sixteen."

He smiled. "Me, too. But I'm terrible at saving my money. You'd better get inside before you freeze to death. The wind is brutal."

"Okay. See you in school," she said, trudging through the snow toward the ski lodge. Serving hot chocolate, coffee, and snacks was much better than standing in the wind all night.

After her shift ended, Amanda waited by the door for her dad to pick her up. He was coming up to the ski resort anyway to pick up guests, so it wasn't out of his way. As she waited, she smiled at Jonas, who'd come to wait by the door, too.

"Are you done for the night?" Amanda asked. Jonas had taken off his ski bibs and stocking cap. She'd never noticed before how thick and wavy his brown hair was or how cute and kind his face looked. In fact, Amanda had hardly noticed Jonas in school at all, even though they'd been going to school together since kindergarten.

"Yeah." He smiled, and his eyes lit up. "I'm waiting for my dad to pick me up."

"Me, too. My dad has to run up here to get guests anyway," Amanda said.

"Do you like working here at the ski resort?" Jonas asked.

"I don't mind it," she said. "It's better than waitressing in a coffee shop, and I couldn't get a job in a clothing store or gift shop." Amanda rolled her eyes. "They all said I was too young."

"That's funny," Jonas said. "I mean, they put you in charge of dangerous machinery here with the ski lift, but you're too young to sell knick-knacks."

She laughed along. "Yeah. It doesn't make any sense."

Her dad drove up in the new van he'd purchased that year, and she waved goodbye to Jonas. Amanda sat in the back so the lodge guests could sit in the middle bench seats. Once they arrived at the lodge and all the other guests had exited the van, Amanda moved to the front seat, and her dad drove her to their house at the back of the property.

"How was work tonight?" Arnie asked his daughter.

"It was okay. But it was really cold out. Luckily, they finally had me come inside and work at the snack shop," Amanda told him.

"I bet it does get cold up there with the wind," Arnie said. "Was that Jonas Nichols I saw you talking to? I didn't know he worked there, too."

"Yeah, it was. He's been there all season like me, but we haven't run into each other until tonight. The owners are always moving the workers around."

Arnie pulled the van up to their home. The lights were on inside, giving off a welcoming glow. "You're mom's home for the night. I'll be back in a bit. Goodnight, sweetheart."

"Goodnight, Dad," Amanda said. She hopped out and headed inside.

After that night, Amanda saw Jonas nearly every time she worked at the ski resort. She wondered if he was making a point of finding her. Not that she minded. They'd talk for a bit, then get back to work. At school, Jonas asked if he could sit with her and her friends at lunch, and she told him that was fine. He got a lot of ribbing from his male friends for sitting with the girls until he pointed out that he was *sitting with the girls!* Then, the other boys asked to sit there, too.

"Do you think I'm bothering you too much?" Jonas asked Amanda one day as they walked to their lockers between classes.

"No. Why?" Amanda was flattered by the attention she

received from Jonas. All her friends thought he was the cutest boy in his group. She thought so, too.

"I thought I heard one of your friends saying, 'There's your boyfriend,' like she thought it was funny. I don't want to embarrass you."

"Oh, she was just teasing me," Amanda said. "My friends are jealous that you pay so much attention to me."

"Oh. Okay."

In March, Jonas turned sixteen. He'd earned enough money to buy an old, beat-up pickup truck. But he was just as proud of it as if it were brand new.

"Would you go out with me on Saturday to celebrate my birthday?" Jonas asked her one day in school. "I mean, if you don't have to work."

"Sure. That would be fun," Amanda said. "I have Saturday off. But wasn't your birthday on Wednesday?"

Jonas shrugged. "I usually work on school nights. So I figured we could go to a movie and then maybe have ice cream."

"Sure." Amanda was excited to go. She only hoped her parents would let her.

"But he just got this driver's license," her father said, sounding nervous. "I'm not sure I want you out in a truck with a brand-new driver."

"It's just from here to town and back again, Dad," Amanda said. "It's not like he's driving me to L.A. or Vegas."

"Vegas! Where'd you get that idea?" a shocked Arnie asked.

"Dad!"

"Oh, honey, let her go with Jonas to the movies," Edna said. "He's a nice boy, and they've known each other forever. They'll be fine."

Arnie grudgingly gave his approval with a ten o'clock curfew.

Amanda and Jonas had a great time, and after that, they saw each other whenever they had the same days off from work. She thought Jonas was not only cute but funny and sweet, too, and he was also a serious student like her.

Once the skiing season had closed for the year, Jonas and Amanda had more time on their hands to spend together. He'd come to the lodge to see her or pick her up. Sometimes Craig, who had just turned eighteen, teased them, but they ignored him. Craig was going into the service voluntarily in the fall, so he had the summer to work and have fun.

One afternoon in April, Edna walked up to Jonas as he sat on one of the sofas in the lodge's living area, waiting for Amanda to finish her shift.

"Are you a good driver?" Edna asked Jonas.

"Uh, yes. I think so," he said. He wondered if Mrs. Burke had heard someone complain about his driving, and he started to worry.

"Do you have a summer job yet?" she asked him.

"No. Not yet. No one is hiring until May," Jonas said.

Amanda had walked up to join them and stood beside Jonas. "Mom. Are you picking on Jonas?"

Edna smiled. "No. I wanted to ask him if he'd like to have a part-time job here over the summer."

Jonas' eyes grew wide. "Really? I'd love to work here."

"That would be great," Amanda said excitedly.

"Well, you may want to know what the job is first." Edna chuckled. "We'd need you to drive guests to and from the airport, the lake, and wherever else they want to go. Plus, you'd also help Arnie with some of the outdoor work, like mowing. How does that sound?"

"It sounds great," Jonas said. "When do you want me to start?"

Edna laughed. "The first day after school ends will be fine."

"Thanks, Mrs. Burke," Jonas said. He couldn't wait for school to end. He loved the lodge and was excited to work there.

As they left to go to the lake, Jonas was all smiles. "I hope you won't mind me working there all summer. I'd hate for you to get tired of me."

"I don't mind at all," Amanda said. "It'll be fun to have someone my own age working there. And we'll see each other all the time."

Both teens were looking forward to a fun summer.

Chapter Eleven

Today – December 29th

Cassie awoke early, showered, and dressed in the lodge's uniform, then headed to the front desk to start her day. There were several guests checking in today for the New Year's Eve holiday, and they had to get the rooms ready. She also had to make sure the order for the food and champagne for New Year's Eve was accurate in case she had to order more.

Jen came in and went immediately to clean rooms while Cassie helped guests check out. Other guests requested spa services, and Cassie made their reservations. As of December 31st, the spa would be closed. And the next day, the entire lodge would shut down unless she sold it.

That thought weighed heavily on Cassie's mind. She should be happy to have such an influential company like Trevor's be interested in purchasing her lodge. But she couldn't help but think that she'd regret it the moment the contract's ink was dry.

"What are you pondering so seriously?" Gabe asked, stopping at the front desk.

"Oh, hi, Gabe. I just have a lot on my mind."

"Don't we all," he said. "I'm on my way to the airport to drop off guests and pick others up."

"Okay." Cassie gazed out the large front window, then came out of her fog. "Say? Would you be able to join us at ten when I give Trevor the tour of the lodge? I think you'd have a lot of input that I wouldn't know."

Gabe scrunched his face as if he'd smelled something rotten. "I don't know, Cassie. Trevor isn't exactly my favorite person, and neither is Blake. I couldn't bear to hear what he'd want to do to this place."

Cassie sighed. "Me, either. That's why I need you to come along. For moral support—and for your knowledge. Please?"

"Okay. But make sure Blake doesn't try to tip me, okay?" Gabe grinned, then walked out the front door.

Ten o'clock came too soon. Trevor, Renee, and Blake had come down for breakfast at nine, and Cassie had made herself scarce. Especially after Blake made a comment about her uniform.

"What on earth are you wearing?" Blake had said. "You look like an average employee, not an owner."

That comment had made her blood boil. "If you own this place, you are an average employee, whatever that means," she snapped back.

Once again, Blake had looked apologetic, but Cassie didn't believe he felt he'd said anything wrong. Otherwise, he wouldn't keep making condescending comments.

Steeling herself, Cassie left Jen in charge of the desk and entered the dining room. "Did you enjoy your breakfast?" she asked Trevor, ignoring Blake.

"It was delicious, although very common fare," Trevor said.

Cassie frowned. They had a buffet breakfast every day for the guests with choices of eggs, bacon, toast, muffins, pastries, cereal, pancakes or waffles, plus fresh fruit and hot and cold beverages. Everyone who stayed there loved the variety. She decided to ignore his comment. If he purchased the lodge, he could serve whatever he wanted.

"Are you ready for your tour?" she asked more cheerfully than she felt.

Trevor stood. "Yes. I'm excited to see the entire place." Renee stood, too, and so did Blake. Renee wore an entirely white ensemble that was supposed to look like a ski outfit but that no one in their right mind would ski in. And her boots were knee-length with heels that had to be five inches tall. Cassie loved heels, too, but Renee's boots were ridiculous for a walking tour.

Gabe entered the dining room just as Cassie doubted he'd show up. She smiled at him gratefully.

"I invited Gabe to come on the tour. He knows this place inside out, so he can answer any questions you have," Cassie said.

Trevor nodded, but Cassie noticed that Blake frowned. Apparently, he wasn't a fan of Gabe's.

"Well, you've already been in the dining room, so let's head through the door into the kitchen," Cassie said. "The kitchen is the full length of the back area of the lodge. Because of the hallway that leads outside, the kitchen is set up in two different areas. This area is mainly a panty, plus a sink, dishwasher, and refrigerator for the morning crew to take care of breakfast. The other section is a full kitchen for making special dinners, or for any type of reception dinner we might book."

"Oh. Do you have weddings and other parties here besides

the free ones?" Trevor asked.

"Yes," Cassie said, leading them across the hallway to the main kitchen. "The dining room will hold a hundred people, but if they need more space, we're always happy to set up the living area for eating too."

"Interesting," Trevor said. "This is a nice kitchen. Definitely updated. How old is this building, and how is the wiring?"

Gabe spoke up. "This main building was built in 1970 after the first lodge burned down. The wiring was replaced once since then in the late '90s when Arnie and Edna did a major remodel on the place. And we also have the electrical certified once a year."

Trevor nodded. Blake slid up next to Cassie and was about to put his arm around her, but she quickly moved toward the back door. "The door leads to an entryway that allows you to go outside or enter the attached building. We have two two-story additions that have several rooms, along with an indoor pool in the middle. At the very end, the long building is the spa. We offer massages, skin services, two steam rooms, one for men and one for women, locker rooms, and also an exercise room for all the guests to use." Cassie led them down the long hallway to the exercise area. They had several treadmills, bicycles, and elliptical machines. "We don't have a weight machine because our insurance frowns on it. Apparently, people get hurt on them."

"It's a nice room," Trevor said, gazing around. "I like that it's all glass so you can see outside while you exercise."

Cassie took them through the different rooms in the spa building. Renee perked up when she saw how serene it looked. "This is nice," she told Trevor.

"Thank you," Cassie said. "The spa was my mother's idea,

and my father thought she was crazy. But from the moment it opened, it's been consistently busy. We also let non-guests book treatments to keep busy. A lot of the locals love coming here."

After that, they stepped outside. Cassie explained about the house hiding at the back of the property and the cottage over to the side, underneath the grove of trees. "That was my grandparents' house until they built the new one. Since then, it has always been the caretaker's house. Gabe's father lived there, and now Gabe does."

"Groundskeeping runs in the family, I see," Blake said, chuckling, but no one else laughed along.

Cassie saw Gabe's jaw tighten. She quickly went to his side. "We couldn't run this lodge without Gabe. He holds this entire place together."

Trevor studied Gabe with interest but didn't reply. "How much land comes with this place?" he asked.

"The place has ten acres," Gabe offered. "It goes all the way back to that tree line, which is past the house and is from that tree over there on the left to right behind the cottage on the right. It's a nice plot of land."

Trevor nodded.

"Would you like to see the house and cottage?" Cassie asked. "You could probably use them as rentals for guests too."

"Yes, I would," Trevor said. Cassie noticed Renee looked bored.

"Okay." Cassie's phone started vibrating in her pocket. She tried to ignore it. "Gabe can drive you in the shuttle bus to see both houses."

Trevor turned to Gabe. "If I buy this place, would you stay on? And would you still want the cottage for your living quarters?"

Gabe shrugged. "We'll have to see if you buy it first."

Trevor grinned. "Good answer."

They all turned and walked into the spa door and through the building toward the front. Cassie's phone had stopped but then started vibrating again. She'd put away her earbuds days ago, no longer wanting to wear them. Pulling her phone out of her pocket, she saw it was Colleen and sighed.

"Shouldn't you answer that?" Blake asked, coming up alongside her.

"Colleen can wait. Showing Trevor around is more important right now."

Blake looked concerned. "Colleen is your client. That's your real job, Cassie. You don't want to risk your job by not answering."

His tone annoyed her. Sure, a week ago, she would have agreed with him, but now, she really didn't care what Colleen's latest issue was. She probably broke a nail or something.

When they passed the front desk, Jen was swamped. Cassie decided she'd better stay behind and help her. "Gabe? Would you show them the house and cottage? Probably the large garage, too. I'll stay here and help Jen."

Gabe nodded, and everyone followed him out to the shuttle bus.

Her phone was driving her crazy, so Cassie finally answered it. "Hi, Colleen. What's up?"

"Why haven't you been answering your phone?" a paranoid-sounding Colleen yelled at Cassie. "Don't you care about me? What if I'd killed myself?"

Then you wouldn't be calling me, Cassie thought, then felt bad. Colleen sounded like she was over the edge, and Cassie didn't want anything to happen to her. "I'm sorry, Colleen,"

Cassie said. "How can I help you?"

Colleen went into a crying fit about how her boyfriend had left her again—right before the big New Year's Eve bash in Times Square, where she was going to be a special guest. She swore she wasn't going to go alone. "You have to go with me. That's your job. You're my PR agent, and you're supposed to be with me at big events," Colleen cried into the phone.

"Can't your assistant go along with you?" Cassie asked. There was no way she could be at the lodge and in New York City at the same time.

"No! I want you. Make it happen, or I'm going to tell your boss you're not doing your job." Collen hung up, which was actually a relief to Cassie.

"Tell him, you little baby," Cassie whispered to herself. Shoving her phone into her pocket, she hurried to the desk to help Jen.

When the group came back inside, Trevor was smiling. If Cassie had to guess, he was pleased with the lodge.

"Would you like me to make dinner reservations for you and your wife for tonight?" Cassie offered, still standing behind the desk.

"Yes. Please. Let's make it a foursome again, if you don't mind," Trevor said. "That way, we can discuss the lodge."

Cassie almost sighed out loud but stopped herself. That would mean another night of Blake cozying up to her, and she just didn't have the energy. She put on a fake smile. "That sounds fine."

"Meanwhile," Trevor said. "Gabe has offered to drive us to the ski resorts so we can see what they're like. He's really a nice guy."

Cassie smiled despite herself. She saw Blake's brow furrow

at the mention of Gabe, but he knew to keep his mouth shut. "Great. Have a nice tour, and I'll see you tonight around seven."

Trevor waved and was followed outside, reluctantly, by Renee and Blake. As they left, Cassie's phone beeped again. "Ugh! Now what?" she said aloud.

Jen stared at her, but Cassie brushed it aside. "Just a client," she said to Jen, then walked away from the desk to answer it. But when she looked at the phone, she was surprised to see the caller was her boss from the PR firm.

"Hello, Jackson. What can I do for you?" Cassie asked. She had a good working relationship with him, so she wasn't too worried.

"I just got off the phone with Colleen Culvers," Jackson said irritably. "Off the record, that woman is nuts!"

"What's going on?" Cassie said, not wanting to agree with him.

"Are you back from that lodge place of yours?" he asked. "Colleen needs someone to hold her hand in New York in two days."

"I'm still in Big Bear," Cassie said. "I'm using my vacation, remember? I'll be back in L.A. on the first of January."

"Not good enough, Cassie. You need to go with Colleen. She won't agree to anyone else escorting her. And before you say another word, I want to remind you that she is our biggest celebrity client. Not just one of them, but THE biggest."

Anger rose inside of Cassie. She'd always gone over and above what should be expected of any employee when it came to her clients. She didn't think she was asking too much to finally have a vacation away from them. "Jackson, I understand she's upset. But there is no reason her personal assistant or another member of our PR firm couldn't escort her to New

York. Personally, I think a woman her age should be able to go there by herself."

"Cassie, celebrities pay us to escort them to events, ensure they have good press, and cover up the bad press. Going with Colleen to an event IS your job," Jackson insisted. "And if she wants you, and only you, to take her, then that's what you will do."

"I'm sorry, Jackson, but I can't. Ask my assistant Marci to go with her. Marci would love to be an associate at the firm. In fact, maybe you should promote her," Cassie said. She couldn't believe those words were coming out of her mouth, yet she couldn't stop herself.

"Excuse me?" Jackson said angrily.

"I meant what I said," Cassie told him. "I've given that firm one hundred and fifty percent the entire time I've worked there. If you can't see yourself clear to let me have two more days of my vacation, then I guess there's nothing else I can say."

"So, what you are saying is to give your position to your assistant, Marcie," Jackson said snidely.

"If that's what you have to do, then do it. Goodbye, Jackson." Cassie hung up. Her heart was pounding furiously in her chest. She couldn't believe she'd just quit her job.

Cassie's phone beeped, and she looked down at it. It was Colleen again. Angrily, Cassie answered the phone. "What now, Colleen?"

"How dare you speak to me that way," Colleen said in her little girl whiny voice.

"Why? It's not like you'd call my boss again and complain, now, would you?" Cassie asked.

"Oh. Well. I didn't mean to cause trouble. I was distraught, Cassie," Colleen said tearfully. "I can't do any of this without you."

"Yes, Colleen, you can. And you should. You're a grown woman with assistants and bodyguards and a whole slew of people who work for you. Your assistant can book your flight and even fly with you. Your agent could go with you. Or your manager. Since I'm no longer responsible for you, Colleen, I'm going to tell you the truth. You're a grown woman who can do anything on her own. Act like it. Stop depending on other people to do everything for you. You have been tough enough to get where you are in a dog-eat-dog industry. So use that toughness and take care of yourself. Now, please don't call me again. Have a great life." Cassie hung up and dropped her phone in her pocket. Good riddance.

After a moment, Cassie realized she was about to sell the lodge, and she no longer had a job. What had she done?

Chapter Twelve

New Year's Eve - 1985

Amanda sat nervously in her bedroom, being careful not to wrinkle her dress or muss her hair. It was her wedding day. To be exact, wedding night because they were getting married on New Year's Eve. She wasn't sure why she was nervous. She'd known Jonas her entire life. They'd been dating on and off since they were fifteen. Still, even at the age of twenty-three, Amanda had a bothersome little doubt in the back of her mind.

Edna opened the door a crack and peeked in. "How are you doing, honey?"

"I'm fine. Nervous, but I'm okay," Amanda said, trying to sound better than she felt.

Edna came into the room and smiled at her daughter. "All brides are nervous, dear."

Amanda knew that, but she still felt uneasy.

Giggling and chatter came from the bedroom next door—Craig's old room that her mother had turned into a sewing room. Her maid of honor and bridesmaids were getting dressed in there. They had all been her best friends in high school, yet Amanda felt like she barely knew them now. After spending four years attending the University of California in Los Angeles, Amanda had grown apart from many of her friends. Once she'd returned home, she'd reconnected with many of them but still felt some invisible distance between them.

With Jonas, though, it had always been easy. After they both graduated high school, he followed her to Los Angeles to attend college. But after two years in the crowded city, Jonas decided he couldn't stay there any longer. L.A. was not the right place for him, and despite being a good student, he hadn't enjoyed college. Reluctantly, he left Amanda behind because she insisted she wanted to finish her business management degree. She loved L.A. and attending college. She had made a few friends and enjoyed going to the beach on the weekends and going out to clubs at night. She liked that it was different than Big Bear and wanted to stay there forever.

By the time Amanda graduated college, though, she wasn't as sure if L.A. was for her. She missed Jonas, even though they'd split up during those two years apart. And she missed her parents. So she went home with her degree in hand and once again started working at the lodge.

Unbeknownst to Amanda, her parents had high hopes for her newly learned abilities. Her mother let Amanda take over the bookkeeping, which Amanda enjoyed doing. They also promoted her to assistant manager of the lodge—which meant she was Jonas' boss. When Jonas had returned from L.A., he'd immediately gone back to his job at the lodge, which he'd always loved. And because they worked near each other, day after day, Amanda and Jonas became a couple again.

And now they were getting married.

"Were you nervous before you married Dad?" Amanda asked her mother.

Edna brought a chair over and sat across from her daughter. "A little. I wanted to marry him, but I also was afraid of 'forever.' What if I couldn't be with him forever? Or what if he got tired of me?" Edna chuckled. "Honestly, honey, there are days you do get tired of each other. But it's the commitment you make that keeps your bond strong."

Amanda looked down at her hands, which were covered in white lace gloves. "Sometimes I miss L.A., and I know if I marry Jonas, we'll never go there again."

"Oh, honey. It's only a couple of hours away. If Jonas hates it so much, you could drive there to visit friends, or I could go with you for an occasional weekend." Edna smiled wide. "I grew up in the L.A. area, remember? I gave it up so your father could have his dream place here."

Amanda knew that they'd moved to Big Bear when she was little, but she'd never heard her mother say that she'd given anything up. "You mean you didn't want to move here?"

"Well, to be honest, not at first. But your father loved it here so much, I figured it wouldn't hurt me to live here too. That's what you do in marriage—you compromise. And it didn't turn out so bad, did it?"

"But were you happy, Mom?" Amanda asked.

"As happy as anyone can be, I suppose," Edna said. "Making life decisions isn't always easy, especially when you're making a big commitment. But if you love each other, then you'll both make compromises throughout your lives. You do love Jonas, don't you?"

"I do," Amanda said. "He's wonderful. And so caring. If I asked him, I know he'd move somewhere else with me to make me happy. But I don't want to do that to him. Yet," she hesitated.

"Yet, you're not sure you want to stay here forever either," Edna said.

"I know you and Dad want Jonas and me to take over the lodge someday, and Jonas is excited about doing that. I'm just not sure if I'm excited about it." Amanda felt close to tears. "But I don't want to disappoint you, or Dad, or Jonas."

Edna reached for her daughter's hands. "Honey. Don't worry about disappointing me or your father. What's important is what you and Jonas want. If you don't want to run the lodge in the future, then don't. I want you to be happy."

"Are you sure?" Amanda asked.

Edna smiled. "Completely sure. And if you don't want to get married tonight, then don't. I never want you to feel like you've been trapped into anything."

Amanda's eyes widened. "I can't back out now. It'll break Jonas' heart. And you and Dad have spent so much on this wedding."

Edna brushed her hand through the air. "None of that matters. If you're not happy, then I'm not happy. Do you want to jump in the car and we'll escape to L.A.? Or maybe even Vegas. I've never been there."

Laughter filled the air. Amanda couldn't imagine her and her mother running away on her wedding day. "That sounds like fun, Mom, but I think I'll stay and get married."

"Are you sure?" Edna asked with a glint in her eyes. "I'm ready to run if you are."

"I'm sure, Mom. But I'll take you up on that offer sometime soon. It would be fun."

"Okay, dear," Edna said. "I love you."

"I love you, too, Mom," Amanda said. The two women stood and hugged.

"Are you feeling better?" Edna asked.

"Yes. I know I'm doing the right thing," Amanda told her.

"Okay, I'll see you out there." Edna smiled warmly. "You look beautiful, sweetie."

"Thanks, Mom."

Edna left just as all the bridesmaids burst into the room and oohed and aahed over Amanda's dress.

Later, as Amanda stood at the top of the stairs that led down into the living area, she suddenly felt relaxed. Her father stood beside her, his arm linked with hers.

"Are you okay?" Arnie asked, looking handsome in his black tuxedo.

"Yeah. I'm okay, Dad," Amanda said calmly. All their guests were seated facing the fireplace and Christmas tree. They included family, friends, and long-time guests who had watched Amanda grow up. Jonas' family was there too. The only one missing was her brother Craig because he was still in the service and stationed in Germany. He hadn't been able to get leave to come home. But everyone else who mattered was there.

Music filled the air, and as her father walked her down the stairs and she looked into Jonas' eyes, a calmness fell over Amanda. She loved Jonas, and that was all that mattered. They'd make a good life together, no matter where they lived. She happily walked toward him and their future.

Chapter Thirteen

Today – December 29th - 30th

Cassie joined Trevor, Renee, and Blake for dinner that evening at a nice seafood and steak restaurant that stood next to Big Bear Lake. Trevor once again commented on the rustic look of the area buildings, but Cassie thought it looked nice. The Christmas lights that trimmed the restaurant's roof reflected in the water, and several pine trees had been decorated with lights, too. It was quaint and cozy, and it felt like home.

After they'd ordered their drinks and food, Trevor spoke up. "I'm not going to mince words or play it cool," he said to Cassie. "I like your lodge, and I want to make an offer."

Blake's face lit up. "Isn't that wonderful, Cassie? You won't have to worry about the place anymore."

"Yes, it is wonderful," Cassie said without much enthusiasm. "But before I get too excited, I'd like to hear your offer."

Trevor smiled. He pulled a notepad from his suit jacket pocket, wrote something on it, and slid it across the table to Cassie.

Cassie picked up the paper and read it. She'd already had

a real estate agent place the lodge on the market, so she knew what the lodge and land were worth. Obviously, Trevor had seen the listing, too, because he offered the exact amount it was listed for.

"Well?" Blake asked, looking as excited as a child at Christmas.

"It's a good offer," Cassie said to Trevor. "I'll give you a card for my real estate agent, and you two can work out the details."

Trevor beamed. "So we have a deal?"

"As far as I can see, yes," Cassie said. This should have been one of the happiest days of her life, but she felt disappointed instead. This kind of money would be a big boon for her brother, Jake, and for her, yet it felt like she was selling a piece of herself.

"Then let's celebrate," Trevor said. He snapped his fingers for the waiter to come and ordered a bottle of champagne. When it arrived and was poured, Trevor lifted his glass. "To the Mountain View Lodge."

Reluctantly, Cassie clinked glasses with everyone.

Gabe picked them up after dinner and looked at Cassie expectantly, but she ignored him. Once they arrived at the lodge, she hurried inside so she wouldn't have to tell him she'd sold the lodge.

Let him sleep one more worry-free night in his cottage, she thought. She knew she wasn't going to get much sleep tonight.

Trevor and Renee said goodnight and went upstairs, but Blake held back.

"There's something I need to tell you," Blake said.

Cassie was surprised at the tone of his voice. He sounded remorseful. "Okay." She led him to a sofa in front of the fireplace, and they sat down. The living area was empty, so they had privacy.

"The band was freaking out that I wasn't going to be with them on New Year's Eve," Blake said. "They're going to be playing for the Times Square New Year's Eve party. It's a big deal."

Cassie nodded. "Colleen Culvers is going to be making an appearance there too. She was upset that I couldn't go with her."

"Really? Then why don't you and I fly out there and be with our clients?" Blake looked excited. "That way, we can still spend New Year's Eve together."

"I'm sorry, Blake, but I told Jen I'd be here to help. It's the last holiday party the lodge will ever put on, and the long-time guests want me here," Cassie said. She didn't want to tell him yet that she'd been fired from her job in L.A. Blake would freak out, but Cassie didn't really care. The more she thought about not working at the PR firm, the happier she felt.

"Okay. I understand," Blake said. He ran his hand through his perfectly combed dark hair. Cassie couldn't help but think how handsome he looked. Yet, his looks no longer affected her the way they used to.

"Trevor is leaving tomorrow on his private plane," Blake said. "I thought I'd ride back to L.A. with him, then book my flight to New York. I know I promised to be here with you, but the band needs me. You understand, don't you?"

Cassie nodded. She'd understood every time he put work before her, just like he had understood when she'd put work before him. But she didn't want to understand anymore. She wanted a relationship that was more than about work. She wanted someone who—at least most of the time—put her first, and she'd do the same. "Go ahead, Blake," she said. "It's probably for the best."

Blake frowned. "What do you mean by that?"

Cassie slid her engagement ring off her finger, reached for Blake's hand, and gently placed the ring in it. "I can't do this anymore. I'm sorry. You're a great guy, and we've had a good time together, but we've been committed to our jobs this whole time, not to each other. Being here the past two weeks has made me see that clearly. I want more than that."

"I don't understand." Blake looked completely confused. "We have everything anyone could want. A beautiful apartment overlooking L.A. High-paying jobs. A great relationship. What more could you want?"

"I want someone who wants to spend time with me. Someone who doesn't put his work first. And I want to do the same. I want to slow down and enjoy life before it passes me by," Cassie said.

Blake shook his head, unable to comprehend her words. "I thought we both had the same goals."

"We did," she said gently. "But now, my views on life have changed. I'm sorry."

Blake looked down at the ring in his hand, then back at her. "I really do love you," he said.

"I loved you, too," Cassie said. "But we no longer want the same things."

He slipped the ring into his pocket. "Will I see you tomorrow before I go?"

"It might be better if we don't see each other," Cassie said. "But I'll fly to L.A. soon and pick up my clothes and personal items. All the furniture and decorations are yours. I just want my things."

He nodded, looking dazed. "Goodbye, Cassie."

"Goodbye, Blake." She reached over and hugged him one

last time. Then she stayed there and watched him walk up the stairs to his room.

She'd lost her job, her relationship, and her lodge all in one night.

* * *

Cassie hid at the house until she was sure Blake had already left for the airport. She knew she was being a coward, but she couldn't help herself. Finally, she walked through the fresh snow that had fallen overnight to the lodge.

"Is it true?" Jen asked as soon as Cassie walked up to the front desk. "Did you sell the lodge to that Trevor guy?"

Cassie was caught off guard. "Where did you hear that?"

"Trevor told me this morning when he was checking out. He said you'd agreed to a price, and he'd be the new owner soon," Jen said. "He even told me I should apply for the manager's position because he'd noticed what a good job I do here."

"Well, he was right about that," Cassie said, smiling at her friend. "You're a great manager here, and you should stay if he wants to keep you on."

"So, it's true?" Jen asked, tears filling her eyes.

"I only agreed on a price. We have a long way to go before signing the paperwork," Cassie said.

"Will we be closing the lodge after New Year's Eve?"

"I think we should stay open if we can retain all our employees. But don't say anything to the staff yet. I need to talk to my real estate agent first, and then I'll make an announcement later today," Cassie said.

"Okay. But I think Trevor told Gabe this morning when he drove them to the airport," Jen said. "When Gabe returned, he looked furious. I haven't seen him since."

Cassie sighed. "I'll go find him." She knew exactly where he'd be.

Cassie walked the short distance from the lodge to the caretaker's cottage. Gabe's truck was sitting outside, so she knew he was there. Softly, she knocked on the hunter-green door.

Gabe opened the door and stared down at her. "You sold the lodge," he said accusingly.

"No papers have been signed yet," Cassie said. "But yes, I agreed to an offer."

Gabe walked away to the kitchen, where he had a bunch of empty boxes. Cassie followed him inside.

"What are all the boxes for?" Cassie asked.

"I'm packing. I'm no longer needed here on January first, remember?" Gabe said.

"But if the deal goes through, the lodge will still be open," Cassie said. "I'm sure you could work for Trevor's company."

Gabe stared at her over a box that sat on the counter. "Trevor already offered me a job. He said I could keep the cottage and still work here, doing everything I've been doing. He even said he'd offer me a raise if I stayed."

"Wow. That's great, isn't it?" Cassie said. She was surprised that Trevor was offering all these jobs to people when he hadn't even signed a single paper.

"Yes. It was really nice of him to offer me my job. But I don't want it," Gabe said.

"Why?" Cassie asked. "You knew that selling the lodge was always the plan. My mother told me to sell it before she died. What difference does it make if you work for me or Trevor?"

"It makes all the difference," Gabe said. He came around the counter and stood in front of Cassie. "I've lived here my entire life. This lodge and cottage are more to me than a job or a place to live. This place was my family. Your mom and dad, you and Jake. You were all like family to me. After my mother died, your mom took me in and watched me so my father could work. She treated me as her own. That's why I stayed here. I could have gone anywhere and worked, but I wanted to stay here—with my family."

Chills ran through Cassie, and tears welled in her eyes. She'd never known that Gabe felt that way. "I'm sorry," she said softly. "But things change. Mom and Dad are gone. My life is somewhere else."

"I know," Gabe said gently. "And I understand. But I can't be here anymore. It won't be the same after you sell it."

Cassie turned around because she didn't want Gabe to see her tears. Everything was changing so quickly. She didn't even have an apartment or a job to return to in L.A. She had no idea what she was going to do. And she hated ruining everyone's life here—the very people she'd known her whole life.

Gabe came up behind her and wrapped his arms around her waist. She leaned into him. Gabe felt warm, strong, and sturdy—something she hadn't felt from a man in a long time.

"Remember that summer before your senior year when we were dating?" Gabe said. "That was the best time of my life. I was crazy about you. I had no idea then that you'd planned on leaving town after graduation. You broke my heart."

"I hadn't meant to," Cassie said. "That was a special time for me, too. But my mother was adamant that I go away to college, so I picked L.A. because it was close."

Gabe dropped a sweet kiss on her cheek and pulled away. Cassie suddenly felt chilled, no longer warmed by his body.

"Well, that's the past. I guess it's time we all move forward,"

Gabe said, returning to packing his kitchen things.

Cassie turned around. "Please don't leave yet, Gabe. Will you at least stay until the lodge is under new ownership? I'm sure Trevor will want the lodge to remain open until he takes it over. And no one other than you and Jen are more capable of keeping this place in order."

He looked at her with his deep brown eyes, and her heart nearly melted. She'd broken it off with Blake, and it would be so easy to fall into Gabe's arms right now. But she couldn't do that to Gabe or to herself. She had to figure out her messed up life first.

"Okay. I'll stay for a few more weeks until Trevor's company takes over, but then I'll be gone," Gabe said.

"Thank you." Cassie watched him a minute. "Where will you go?"

He smiled. "Not far. Both ski resorts have already offered me jobs, and that big resort on the lake says they'll double what the ski resorts offer. So don't worry about me. Apparently, I'm in demand."

"Honestly, it doesn't surprise me," Cassie said, smiling.

"Are you still staying for the New Year's Eve party tomorrow night?" Gabe asked.

"Of course," Cassie said quickly. "Blake left to babysit the band, but I'll be here."

Gabe shook his head. "Blake is an idiot. Choosing work over you? Only an idiot would do that."

"Yeah, well," Cassie said, unsure how to reply. "So, you have me to pick on for two more days. Do you think you can handle that?"

Gabe grinned. "You bet."

Cassie left Gabe to his packing with a hole in her heart. She hated thinking of Gabe living anywhere else but in the cottage. That was his home. But she was happy he'd been offered so many job choices. It was weird, though, thinking of the lodge without Gabe.

She went back to the lodge and took over for Jen at the front desk. When she wasn't busy with guests, Cassie called her real estate agent and told her about the offer she'd been given and gave her Trevor's number. Just as she was about to start keying the receipts into the computer, her phone beeped.

Cassie looked at it and sighed, then answered. "Colleen. I told you not to call me. I don't work for the firm anymore."

Colleen apologized profusely and told Cassie that she'd called Jackson and told him if they didn't hire her back, she'd find a new PR firm.

"What?" Cassie was shocked.

"I thought really hard about what you said to me the other day," Colleen told Cassie. "You were so right. I need to stop depending on everyone else and grow up. No one has ever talked to me like that before. I needed to hear it. And I still want you to be my PR agent. I promise, if you go back to work there, I won't be such a clingy, whiny brat."

Cassie couldn't help but laugh at the last words. "I'd love to represent you, Colleen, but Jackson fired me. I doubt he'll take it back."

"Oh, he will. Believe me. You'll get a call from him really soon," Colleen said.

They talked a little more and then hung up. Cassie didn't know how she felt about it all. She needed a job but wasn't sure she wanted to babysit celebrities and sports stars any longer. Before she could collect her thoughts, her phone beeped again. It was Jackson.

"Listen, Cassie. I'll get right to the point," Jackson said. "I shouldn't have been so rash and fired you the other day. I think we both were in a weird place and not thinking straight. I hope you'll ignore that conversation and come back to work. Your clients adore you, and I know you're an amazing public relations manager."

"I don't know, Jackson," Cassie said. "I'm not sure I want to work there anymore. I'm on call 24/7 with clients, and I never have a life. Things would have to change."

"Fine. Fine. We can place boundaries on your clients and have a backup they can call when you have time off," Jackson said. "Whatever you want, Cassie. And I'm willing to raise your salary as well. How does double what you're already making sound?"

She gasped. Double? That was insane. Jackson must really want to keep Colleen happy. "Can I think about it, Jackson? I'll be here for two more days, and then I'll be heading home."

"Sure. Yeah. Think about it, and then please say yes."

"I'll talk to you when I get back into town," Cassie said. When they hung up, Cassie was still in shock. Double her salary. With that, she could rent her own high-rise apartment in L.A. But it would mean that she'd still never have a life of her own.

Or maybe never have the life she really wanted deep down inside.

Cassie had a lot of soul-searching to do.

Chapter Fourteen

Christmas Eve 2000

"So, what do you kids think?" Arnie said, looking first at Amanda and then at Jonas. Even though Amanda was thirty-eight years old, her father still called her kid.

"Are you sure you want to retire?" Amanda asked her father. "You love the lodge."

"I do love the lodge," Arnie said. "But I'm getting old and tired. And," he smiled over at his wife, Edna. "I promised your mom that we'd do some traveling and enjoy life a little before we get too old."

Edna nodded. "He did," she said, smiling. "Besides. You two have been working for us for too long. It's time to turn the tables. We'll still help out when we're here. We just won't be running the place anymore."

"And the house comes with the lodge," Arnie said. "Of course, we still need a place to live." He chuckled. "But we can switch places. You can have the big room upstairs, and we'll take the small suite of rooms downstairs. We shouldn't be climbing those stairs anyway."

Amanda glanced over at her husband, Jonas, who was all smiles. She knew he'd been waiting for the day when they could purchase the lodge from her parents. They'd been saving their money for years, and since they didn't have to pay a mortgage or rent, they'd been able to save a lot. Now, they could put a big down payment on the lodge, which would go to her parents' retirement account, and make monthly payments to them as well. It was the perfect way for Arnie and Edna to retire but still be affordable for her and Jonas.

"Well, I suppose it won't be much different than now," Amanda said. "Except you two will leave once in a while."

"And you and Jonas will have full control of the lodge and the house," Arnie said.

Amanda's brows rose. "Full control?"

"Absolutely," Edna said. "We won't say a word, even if you paint the lodge purple. It's your lodge and your house. We'll just be part-time employees from now on."

Amanda laughed. "Okay. Remember you said that, Mom."

"We're just happy you want to keep the lodge in the family," Arnie said, standing to hug his daughter. "Your brother loves Florida and wants nothing to do with this place. We're happy he's happy, but we're even happier that you and Jonas want the lodge."

It was the day of their Christmas Eve celebration, and they were in the lodge's living area near the big fireplace. Tonight would be the busiest night of the year, and the employees were bustling to finish everything.

"You aren't leaving us during the holidays, are you?" Amanda asked, suddenly scared she'd have to run the celebrations by herself. With two children, Cassie, age nine, and Jake, age thirteen, along with a full-time job at the lodge, Amanda wasn't sure she could manage the holidays alone.

"No, we won't abandon until the holidays are over," Edna said. "This place is crazy right now. But we thought we'd do some traveling after the first of the year. I've always wanted to see the national parks around the country and go out east. I wouldn't mind going to Florida, either. I just want to see things before I get too old."

"I don't blame you," Amanda said. She had always wanted to travel, too, but the lodge and her kids kept her busy. Hopefully, her time would come, too."

That night, all the regulars and a few new guests were downstairs for the Christmas Eve dinner and the celebration in the living area. Champagne was served all around, and before it got too out of hand, Arnie stood by the fireplace and made an announcement.

"We want to thank all of you for being here, especially those of you who've come each year since we opened this lodge in 1965. I'm so happy to announce that our daughter, Amanda, and her husband, Jonas, who've you known practically their entire lives, will be taking over the lodge."

The guests all smiled and clapped.

"So, let's all raise a glass to the new owners of the Mountain View Lodge," Arnie said.

The entire room raised their glasses and congratulated the couple. Afterward, while Edna played holiday songs on the piano and others sang along, many guests came up to Amanda and Jonas and congratulated them.

George Henley, whom Amanda had known since she was five, hugged her. "Congratulations. This place is in good hands."

"Thanks, George," Amanda said. He was now married and

had children of his own, and they still came every year for Christmas, just as his parents had done.

Gifts were passed around to the young children in the room, and everyone had a wonderful time. Amanda always looked forward to the holidays because they were the most special time of the year at the lodge. It was work, but it was also fun because most of the people who came had become like family.

That evening, after everyone had returned to their rooms and the lodge was quiet, Amanda and Jonas sat on the sofa by the fireplace.

"Can you believe it?" Jonas said, smiling at his wife. "It's finally ours."

"We always knew it would be at some point," Amanda said. She smiled back. "I know that was your dream. I'm happy it came true."

Jonas watched her a moment. "Are you happy?"

She was taken aback by his question. "Of course. Why wouldn't I be?"

"Well, I know it hasn't always been your dream to own the lodge. Or even to live in Big Bear your whole life," Jonas said.

Amanda thought a moment before replying. Yes, there was a time when she would have loved to move to L.A. and maybe live near the ocean. But that had been so long ago, and she'd been so busy raising a family and working over the past fifteen years that she hadn't spent much time thinking about anything else.

"I am happy," she finally said. "Yes, I enjoyed living in L.A. when I went to college, but I was young. You want to do exciting things when you're young. But I came back, and I married you, not because I had no other choice but because I wanted to. I love you, Jonas. And I love our children and our life. Is it hard sometimes? Definitely. But we have a good life here."

Jonas reached over and kissed her sweetly on the lips. "Someday, we'll travel too," he said. "I know you'd like to. But for now, let's make the lodge our own. And the house, too. We do have a good life."

"We do," she said softly. And they sat by the fire until all that was left were the burning embers.

Chapter Fifteen

Today - New Year's Eve

New Year's Eve was always a hectic time at the lodge, and this year was no different. Cassie had announced to the staff the day before that the lodge was going to have a new owner. She asked everyone to please stay on so they could remain open until the new owner took possession.

There were mixed feelings among the staff. Many were happy to still have a job, while others felt the place would never be the same under a new owner.

"It won't have that homestyle feel anymore," Jen said, echoing what other staff members were saying. "I'm sure they will change things, and it'll feel more like a chain resort than a local one."

Cassie couldn't deny that wasn't true. It bothered her, too, knowing that Trevor would change things to make more money. Like charging extra for the Christmas and New Year's celebrations and possibly overcharging for the rooms so the regulars could no longer afford to stay.

"But you'll still be here," Cassie told Jen. "And hopefully, many of the staff will stay. That's what will make it feel like a hometown lodge."

"But you won't be here," Jen said sadly. "All this ends with you."

Cassie's heart sank. She knew that was true, but she wasn't sure what to do about it. She hugged Jen, then returned to work preparing for the holiday dinner and dancing in the living area. Tonight, they'd hired a three-piece band to play music to dance to, and even the children were excited.

After checking on how dinner was going and making sure everything looked perfect, Cassie walked to her house to change clothes. The sun had already gone down, and the night was cold. Gabe had shoveled the new snow off the walkways and road, so it wasn't too bad of a walk. There were also old-fashioned-looking streetlights that lined the road so she could see on her way home.

Home, Cassie thought as she unlocked the door and walked inside. It was chilly, so she stacked wood in the fireplace and started it, enjoying the crackling sound and feeling the warmth immediately. Someone had brought wood into the house for her these past two weeks, and she knew who that someone was. Gabe. He always thought of everyone else's needs, even though he'd never let on that he did.

Cassie looked around the house, remembering when she was a child and her grandparents, parents, and she and Jake lived here together. She was eleven when her mother and father bought the lodge from her grandparents, and she remembered how her parents had switched rooms in the house with her grandparents. It had seemed odd at the time, but now, she understood why. Her parents had bought the house and lodge, and her grandparents wanted them to feel like they owned it.

Cassie remembered the good times, like birthday celebrations when her grandmother would bake and decorate a cake for her and Jake and Christmas morning at the house before her parents' workday began. But she also remembered the sad times. She remembered the day her father died in 2010 in a car accident on the slippery roads. She was nineteen and in her first year of college in L.A. Her grandmother Edna had called her and told her to come home, and Cassie was on the first flight out. She remembered her mother was inconsolable, and her grandmother and grandfather had immediately taken over running the lodge so Amanda could grieve. Then, a year later, her grandfather Arnie had died of a heart attack in the downstairs bedroom. Cassie had been home from college, and they were all eating breakfast before going to work when her grandmother commented that it was odd that Arnie wasn't up yet. She found him in bed, gone, and again the family grieved.

Edna and Amanda, mother and daughter, ran the lodge together after that with the help of Gabe and his father, Mitch. Cassie's mother had been even more adamant that Cassie choose a different path in life than owning the lodge. At the time, Cassie had thought that her mother was just sad because both her father and her husband were gone. Now, she understood why her mother wanted her to have more. Running the lodge was hard work. It took every moment of your life to keep it going.

But the life Cassie had built away from Big Bear wasn't necessarily the life she wanted either.

Cassie showered and dressed in the last nice gown she'd brought along just for New Year's Eve. It was a strapless royal blue gown made of satin with a light smattering of glittery rhinestones swirling around it. She put her blond hair up and used bobby pins with tiny rhinestones so her hair would sparkle like her dress. A touch of make-up brightened her eyes and lips. It was the last New Year's Eve party she'd ever host at the lodge, and she wanted to make it the best one ever.

Just as she put on a long, black wool coat that had once belonged to her mother, there was a knock at the door. Cassie went to answer it and wasn't surprised to see Gabe standing there.

"I thought you might need a ride to the lodge tonight," he said, looking very handsome in a black suit and tie.

"Thank you," Cassie said, grabbing her small black bag. "These heels weren't meant for the snow."

He smiled, and a delicious chill ran down Cassie's spine. He looked like he'd just had his hair cut, and his beard was groomed, too. There was nothing backwoods or small-town about Gabe tonight. He was as handsome as any millionaire she'd known in L.A.

They walked out into the night, and she saw immediately that he wasn't driving his truck. "Mom's car," Cassie said, seeing the black Ford Explorer sitting there.

"I hope you don't mind," Gabe said, opening the passenger door for her. "I didn't think you'd want to climb up into my truck in an evening gown."

She smiled at him. "I don't mind at all."

They drove the short distance to the lodge and entered through the front door. Cassie took off her coat, with Gabe's assistance, and hung it on the rack in the entryway. When she turned back to Gabe, she heard him whistle softly.

"You look beautiful," he said. "Absolutely perfect."

She drew in a breath, not knowing how to respond. The way he looked at her said it all. She only smiled at him, and they walked into the lodge together.

"You look so beautiful!" Jen exclaimed, coming up to Cassie. "And Gabe. Who knew you cleaned up so well?"

"You look lovely too," Cassie told Jen. She wore a dark green gown with a sweetheart neckline and cap sleeves. "It's always fun to dress up for New Year's Eve."

Jen nodded. Her husband was by her side, and Jen's children, looking adorable in a small suit and a dress, were running around the living area as the band set up against the wall near the fireplace.

"Well, shall we go in and have dinner?" Cassie said. Jen called for the children, and they all entered the dining room and took their seats at the tables where place cards showed their names.

It was a lovely evening. The dinner was perfect, and Cassie particularly enjoyed having Gabe beside her and Jen near her, too. Once everyone had served themselves at the buffet, Cassie stood.

"Thank you all for another wonderful holiday season here at the Mountain View Lodge," she began. "I see so many familiar faces here, and I thank you for being a part of our family since as long as I can remember. I also want to welcome the newcomers this year. I hope you have enjoyed your stay as much as we enjoy having you here." She smiled at the large room full of people. "I have an announcement to make. The lodge is in the process of being sold, so that means we won't be closing on January first as we had planned. The lodge will be open until the new owners take control of it. That also means you can book a room for next year because we know the lodge will be open."

The people looked both happy and sad to hear the place

had been sold. Cassie knew the regulars would be sad to see the lodge no longer owned by her family, and the new guests might be happy to be able to return.

George stood at his table with his glass in his hand. "I'm sorry to see you go, Cassie," he said. He lifted his glass. "Here's to so many wonderful memories, decades of memories, your family has given ours, and so many others, during the holidays."

Everyone stood and raised their glasses to the toast. "Here, here!" they all yelled.

Cassie raised her glass in George's direction with tears in her eyes. "Thank you, George. Thank you, everyone," she said, her voice cracking. The entire room clinked glasses, and then everyone sat down again.

Gabe leaned over and placed his arm around Cassie. "Are you okay?"

She nodded as she wiped her eyes. "Who knew leaving this place would be so hard?"

"I did," he whispered to her, then kissed her tenderly on the cheek.

They ate dinner, and soon, everyone drifted into the living area where the band started playing a soft, slow tune. Cassie tried to help the staff clean up the dining room, but they all told her to enjoy her evening. Reluctantly, she went into the living area and joined Jen and some of the other staff who had the night off.

The sofas and chairs, along with the rugs, had been moved to the side of the room, leaving a large area for dancing. As the room filled with guests, the music became more lively. Couples danced while children joined in, copying their parents' moves. Cassie stood to the side happily watching everyone enjoy the evening. For thirty-two years of her life, she'd been a part of this celebration, along with the Christmas parties, Fourth of July celebrations, Halloween dress-up nights, and family Thanksgiving evenings. Her grandparents and parents had always done their best to make the guests feel welcome and like family. Now, she wasn't sure how the new owners would treat the guests. Would they make each guest feel special? Or just like any other guest at any other resort. That thought made her sad.

"Dance with me," Gabe said, coming up beside Cassie and offering his hand.

Cassie accepted his hand and followed him to the dance floor, where he drew her into his arms, and they swayed to the music.

"You're going to miss this, aren't you?" he asked, looking into her eyes.

"The lodge or dancing with you?" she teased.

"Both," he said, holding her closer. They moved in perfect rhythm as if they'd been dancing together their entire lives.

"Blake should be here dancing with you," Gabe said in her ear. "But I'm glad he's not because then I can have all your dances."

Cassie pulled back slightly and looked at him. "Blake and I aren't together anymore. We didn't want the same things."

"I should say I'm sorry," Gabe said. "But to tell the truth, I'm not." He grinned. "You deserve much better than him."

Cassie didn't answer. So many feelings were swirling inside of her that she couldn't make sense of them. Gabe made her feel safe and cared for, and the lodge was her home. But she also knew she was just feeling nostalgic about the past.

"What things do you want?" Gabe asked.

Cassie looked up at him, confused. "What?"

"You said you and Blake didn't want the same things. So, what do you want, Cassie?"

You, was Cassie's first thought, but she didn't say it out loud. She couldn't think straight, being so close to Gabe. "I don't know yet, to tell you the truth," she answered.

"Then tell me when you do know, okay?" he said tenderly.

The music changed to a snappier tune, and guests started coming up to Cassie to express their feelings about the lodge changing hands or to thank her for all the years they've enjoyed coming there. Gabe disappeared in the crowd, and Cassie forced herself to smile and talk to the many people who approached her.

Midnight drew closer. Many of the children who'd wanted to stay up had fallen asleep on the sofas around the room. Jen had left with her family to put the kids to bed, and some of the other people had gone to their rooms, tired from the fun night. The staff filled flutes with champagne to celebrate the magical midnight hour.

Thirty seconds before midnight, the band announced for everyone to find the one they loved. Out of nowhere, Gabe showed up at Cassie's side with two glasses of champagne.

The countdown began: ten, nine, eight. Cassie turned and looked up into Gabe's familiar eyes. She wasn't sure of much right now, but one thing she knew for certain. His warm brown eyes could easily persuade her to stay with just a look.

"Happy New Year!" everyone yelled and clinked glasses, and the band started playing Auld Lang Syne.

"Happy New Year," Gabe said softly, clinking his glass to hers.

"Happy New Year," Cassie said.

Gabe bent down and placed a soft kiss on Cassie's lips.

"I hope you find what you're looking for," he said quietly. He kissed her again, then turned and walked out of the lodge.

Cassie's heart was a mess.

Chapter Sixteen

This Past June

Amanda lay in the hospital bed they had set up in the first-floor bedroom at the house. She knew she didn't have much time left. Six months prior, she'd been diagnosed with stage 4 cervical cancer. It had spread so far throughout her body that she'd decided against treatment since it wouldn't have saved her anyway. She chose instead to manage the pain and symptoms with medicine and live out her life as best she could.

Now, her life was almost over.

"Hey, Mom. How are you feeling?" Cassie asked as she entered the room.

Amanda smiled up at her daughter. Cassie had been coming every weekend since Amanda had been diagnosed, except when she had to work. Recently, Amanda had hired two full-time nurses—one for nighttime and one for the day—to help care for her. But having Cassie there meant the world to her.

"I'm doing okay," Amanda said, setting down the book she'd been trying to read. Her attention span wasn't what it used to be, and she often fell asleep while reading.

"Are you in any pain?" Cassie asked. "I think you're due for a pill if you need it."

Amanda shook her head. "Those things make me fuzzy. I'll wait as long as I can to take one."

Cassie frowned. "Just don't wait until you're in major pain. The doctor said it's easier to manage the pain when you take the pills on time instead of taking them after you're in excruciating pain."

"Yes, dear, I know," Amanda said. "I promise I won't wait too long." She watched her daughter nod. She was so proud of Cassie. Not only had her daughter gone off to college, but she now worked for a prestigious public relations firm and managed several famous clients. She was happy Cassie had moved on, like Jake had, and not stayed working at the lodge.

"Come sit down and tell me about your life," Amanda said.

Cassie sat on the chair beside the bed. "You know my life better than I do, Mom," she said, chuckling. "There's nothing new except that I babysit spoiled clients 24/7."

"It must be exciting, though," Amanda said. "You get to go to red carpet events and dress up. It's more fun than managing the desk at the lodge."

Cassie shrugged. "I don't mind working the desk here. I love the lodge."

"Oh, please," Amanda said, waving her frail hand through the air. "Hearing customers complain all day and running around trying to make everyone happy is not fun."

"Well, you just described what I do for my clients," Cassie said, laughing.

"Promise me you won't hesitate to sell the lodge once I'm gone," Amanda said. "I don't want you to keep it out of some kind of family loyalty. Jake doesn't want to come back here and run it, and you shouldn't have to either."

"But Mom, this lodge was your life," Cassie said, looking confused. "How can you say I should get rid of it?"

Amanda sighed. "Because you should. Honey, I personally didn't want to take over the lodge and run it, but your father just loved it so much. He loved everything to do with Big Bear, and because I loved him, I stayed. But it's so much work, and after your father died, it's been even harder to keep up. I don't want you to keep it just because you think you have to."

"Okay, Mom," Cassie said soothingly. "I wouldn't be able to run it and keep my job anyway, so if you want me to sell, I will. But I'll miss the lodge. It's my home."

"I know, Cass. But soon, you and Blake will be married, and you'll make a home of your own. All I want is for you to be happy," Amanda said.

Cassie nodded her agreement.

"I think I'll take one of those pain pills now," Amanda said, suddenly feeling very tired. Cassie gave her one with a glass of water, and she swallowed it. Soon, she drifted off to sleep, content in the knowledge that her daughter would have a happy future.

Chapter Seventeen

Today – New Year's Day

Cassie left on an early morning flight to L.A. The night before, Gabe had left her mother's car out in front of the lodge for her, so she drove it to Big Bear Airport with instructions for Jared or Gabe to pick it up. She hadn't wanted to see anyone before she left—especially Gabe. Saying goodbye would have been heartbreaking.

After landing in L.A., Cassie took a cab from the airport to the high-rise apartment she shared with Blake. She asked the concierge if they had any boxes for packing, and he said he'd send them up right away. Once upstairs, Cassie set her suitcase down and walked to the large floor-to-ceiling windows.

The view from the living room was spectacular at night, but today, it was hazy with smog and not so pretty. The traffic noise filtered up from the street below, and the other buildings around theirs didn't offer the privacy one would expect. She saw a woman across the way doing yoga in her living room and a man sitting at his dining room table drinking coffee. Cassie rarely spent any time in the apartment during the day and had never noticed these things before. Or maybe she'd ignored them on purpose.

Someone knocked on the door, and she answered it. The concierge had sent up several empty boxes. She tipped and thanked the kid who worked in the building and then headed to the bedroom.

On the plane ride there, Cassie had done some deep soul-searching about what she wanted out of life. And by the time she'd ridden to the apartment in the crushing city traffic, she'd made up her mind. She'd called Jackson and thanked him for the offer but said she wasn't going to return to her job.

"I highly recommend Marcie James," she'd told Jackson. "She knows these clients as well as I do, and they know her. She'd be a perfect fit."

Jackson had tried talking her into coming back, but she stood her ground. Cassie had decided what she really wanted—where she absolutely belonged—and nothing was going to change her mind.

She packed the items she wanted to keep—clothing, pictures, trinkets—and then packed the rest for Goodwill. She'd ask the concierge to take the boxes there for her and would tip them well to do it. Those boxes held many of her designer suits, dresses, and shoes that she wouldn't need where she was going. She knew she could have sold them for a lot of money at a high-end thrift shop, but she didn't want to bother. Maybe someone with a new job but little money could use her clothes to start their career. She hoped so.

Two suitcases and four boxes later, she called the concierge to come up and help her bring the things down to pack up her car. It surprised her that after living together for two years, she had so little that she wanted to take with her.

Cassie settled in a nice hotel with her two suitcases, leaving the boxes in the car. Tomorrow, she'd sell her car—a new, shiny white sports car—to a car dealership and ship the boxes. She wouldn't need the car where she was going. Then she'd take a plane out of L.A. Cassie was excited to begin her new life.

* * *

The next afternoon, the plane Cassie had taken out of LAX arrived at the small airport. She waited for a cab and then told them the address of her destination. As they winded through the small-town streets, Cassie smiled. She'd never been so happy to be away from the bustling big city.

As her destination came into focus, her heart beat faster. This was her life. This was where she belonged. Once the car stopped, she paid the cab driver, pulled out her two suitcases, and stepped inside the warm, cozy lodge.

"Cassie?" Jen looked up from the front desk and smiled widely. "I didn't expect you back so soon!" She ran around the desk and hugged Cassie tightly.

"I guess I just couldn't stay away," Cassie said, laughing.

Pulling away, Jen looked at her. "Are you here to clean out the house before Trevor takes over?"

"No," Cassie said. "I'm here to run the lodge."

"What?" Jen looked confused.

"I didn't sell the lodge after all," Cassie said. "I couldn't. I love this place as if it were a member of my family. So I'm staying."

"Oh, Cassie!" Jen hugged her again. "I'm so happy!"

"Me, too," Cassie said, smiling. "I belong here."

Jen pulled away. "You do. This is your legacy. Your parents

and your grandparents would be so proud."

"Thanks, Jen," Cassie said. "So, I think the first order of business should be to draft a letter to all our regular customers to tell them that the lodge is no longer selling to an outsider and we'd love to have them here for our annual Christmas Eve and New Year's Eve celebrations."

"I'm on it," Jen said, running around the desk to the computer. "Everyone will be thrilled."

Cassie glanced around. "Is Gabe here?"

Jen smiled at her friend. "Yes, he is. The last I saw him, he said he'd be in room 217 fixing the shower. Apparently, there was a leak."

"I'll go tell him I'm here," Cassie said, excited to see Gabe's face when he saw her. She walked up the stairs and headed down the hallway. The door to 217 was open, so she stepped inside then entered the bathroom. Gabe was standing on the edge of the tub with a wrench in his hand, tightening the shower head as it dripped water.

"What's the matter? Can't you fix a little water leak around here?" Cassie teased him.

Gabe turned so fast that he wrenched the shower head in the wrong direction, and water sprayed him right in the face. He said a few choice words as he tried to get out of the water's spray.

Cassie laughed and grabbed one of the towels off the rack, handing it to him as he stepped down from the tub.

Gabe toweled off his hair and face, then looked at Cassie with a stunned expression. "Why are you here?"

She smiled at him. "I came home."

Gabe stared at her a moment, then drew closer. "You're not selling the lodge?"

Cassie shook her head. "No. I'm going to own it. I'm your new boss. Do you think you can handle that?" She grinned.

Gabe grinned back. "I think I can handle that." He reached for her, and she stepped into his arms as he dropped his lips onto hers.

Cassie had never felt more at home than she did right now.

Epilogue

One Year Later – New Year's Eve

Cassie sat in one of the lodge's rooms on the second floor as Jen fussed with her dress. A year after coming home for good, she and Gabe were getting married. She wasn't nervous at all and wasn't second-guessing her decision. Everything in her life felt right. Gabe was the perfect choice for her.

Just as her parents had done before her, Cassie and Gabe were getting married on New Year's Eve so their regular guests could join in on the celebration. Many had been here when her parents married, and some of the new regulars were excited to join in on the celebration. A new year, a new life together, a new beginning. Cassie couldn't wait to see what the future held for her and Gabe.

"Are you ready?" Jen asked, smiling at her friend.

"I am," Cassie said. She wore a white satin, V-neck gown with a lace bodice and shoulder straps. Sequins lightly decorated the dress and glittered in the light when she moved. The dress had a small train, and her waist-length veil was held in her hair with a sequined comb. It was simple yet elegant, and

Cassie looked beautiful.

As they waited for their cue, Cassie thought of her mother and grandmother. Both had gone before her as owners of the lodge—sometimes reluctantly. She remembered how her grandmother Edna reminisced about her youth on the coast of California and how her life had changed when Arnie bought the lodge. And then her mother, Amanda, had come home and married Jonas, even though she, too, had loved southern California and had wanted so much more. But in the end, they both had seemed happy with their decisions. Cassie wondered if they had been as sure of their decisions as she was. Despite her mother's attempt to give Cassie a different life, Cassie had chosen to come back. She knew this was what she wanted, and this was where she belonged. The lodge made her happy, which was all her mother wanted for her. Cassie hoped her mother, somewhere in Heaven, would understand.

There was a knock on the door, and Jen opened it. Standing there in a black tux was George Henley. "Are you ready?" he asked.

Cassie nodded. She'd asked George to walk her down the aisle because he was the closest to her father of anyone else who came to the lodge. They walked out to the top of the stairs as George's wife, Becky, began to play Mendelssohn's Wedding March on the piano.

Cassie's brother, Jake, stood in front of her and smiled. "Who knew you two would end up together," he teased, then kissed her lightly on the cheek. Then Jake escorted Jen down the staircase, following Jen's two children, who played the part of flower girl and ring bearer.

"Don't let me fall down the stairs and ruin your moment," George teased Cassie, winking. Then, seriously, he said, "I'm so proud to stand in for your father."

Cassie held back tears as she smiled at him. She was happy to include such a good friend in her special day.

Together, Cassie and George descended the staircase as the guests stood. He guided her down the aisle toward Gabe, looking handsome in a black tuxedo, standing in front of the stone fireplace. Staring into his warm brown eyes, Cassie knew, at last, she was home.

~ *End* ~

About the Author

Deanna Lynn Sletten is the author of *Mrs. Winchester's Biographer, The Secrets We Carry, The Ones We Leave Behind, The Women of Great Heron Lake, Miss Etta, Finding Libbie,* and several other titles. She writes heartwarming women's fiction, historical fiction, a murder mystery series, and romance novels with unforgettable characters. She has also written one middle-grade novel that takes you on the adventure of a lifetime.

Deanna is married and has two grown children. When not writing, she enjoys peaceful walks in the woods around her home with her beautiful Aussie—Miss Etta, traveling, photography, and relaxing on the lake.

To learn more about Deanna and her books, connect with her at: www.deannalsletten.com

Printed in Great Britain
by Amazon

31654497R00089